Mint Tea and Murder

A Cozy Mystery in Morocco

(Whispering Pines Cozy Mysteries: Book 6)

D1710424

Mint Tea and Murder

A Cozy Mystery in Morocco

(Whispering Pines Cozy Mysteries: Book 6)

PENELOPE LOVELETTER

LOVELETTER
PUBLICATIONS

EST. 2022

Other Books by Penelope Loveletter

Whispering Pines Cozy Mysteries:

Whispers of Murder
Whispers of Death
Whispers of Mystery
Whispers in the Dark
Macarons and Murder
Meringues and Murder
Mint Tea and Murder

Agatha and Christie Cozy Mysteries:

The Snow Globe Murder

Whispering Pines Sweet Romances:

Whispers by the Lake
Whispers of the Heart
Whispers of Forever

Dedicated to my parents,

Kent and Gayle Crookston—

Thank you

♡

mosque, public oven, and hammam - that's a traditional bathhouse."

"Em. That's fascinating. But my feet are killing me. The hotel?"

"Right." She looked down at her phone, brushing her wavy red hair over her shoulder. "It's this way. I've just read so much about this place, I can't believe we get to actually be here!"

He grinned and took her hand. "I hear you. This is amazing."

They passed an open doorway where an elderly craftsman bent over an intricate piece of metalwork, his tools clinking out a rhythmic melody as he carved a brass tabletop. A few streets further on, a weaver's fingers danced across a loom, threads of wool transforming into a colorful rug.

"Look at that woodcarving!" Emma tugged Daniel's sleeve, pointing to an ornate cedar door with geometric patterns. "Did you know that Islamic artisans developed these incredible geometric designs because their faith discouraged depicting living things in art?"

"Really." Daniel nodded and glanced pointedly at Emma's phone. "Do you want me to navigate?"

"No. I've got this." She picked up the handle of her suitcase and stared walking again.

The alley opened into a small square where a group of children kicked a soccer ball, their laughter echoing off the high walls. The call to
2

prayer floated down from a nearby minaret, its haunting melody mixing with the shouts of vendors and the distant bleating of a goat.

"Are you sure this is the most direct route?" Daniel asked.

"The maze-like layout was intentional," Emma explained as they turned down another winding passage. "It helped protect the city from invaders - if you didn't know your way around, you'd get completely lost."

Despite his exhaustion, Daniel laughed. "I don't know if it's just because I didn't sleep on the flight, but I think the plan was effective."

A cart laden with fresh mint and fragrant pink roses rolled past, the vendor calling out in Arabic. Emma inhaled deeply, savoring the sweetness mixed with the dry desert air as they turned down a narrow dead-end alley.

"And we're here!"

In front of them was a beautiful archway surrounding two enormous carved wooden doors and a tiled sign in both Arabic and English reading Hotel al Zuhur.

Daniel opened the door and Emma stepped inside and gaped. Intricate geometric patterns had been carved into the plaster ceiling and rays of late afternoon sun filtered through the windows, casting shadows across the mosaic-stone tiled floor.

"Welcome, welcome!" A tall man in an embroidered *djellaba,* a traditional Moroccan robe, swept forward, arms outstretched. "I am Mustafa, and this is my hotel. You must be Emma and Daniel."

Emma nodded, still taking in the ornate room.

"Your timing is perfect," Mustafa said. "You have come at the perfect day. Tonight we have something special planned - a true Moroccan evening." He led them across a courtyard to a salon. Carved wooden screens separated intimate seating areas where guests lounged on poufs and low cushioned benches. The scent of mint tea and orange blossoms filled the air.

Several other hotel guests were already seated on the low couches that ran along the edges of the room. Emma stared at the mosaic tiled walls, potted palms, and then at the carved plaster ceiling.

"This is amazing!" she whispered.

In one corner, a musician sat cross-legged on an embroidered cushion, his fingers dancing across the strings of an instrument Emma didn't recognize. His haunting melody floated through the room.

"That is Karim," Mustafa gestured, noticing Emma's gaze. "He plays the oud - traditional Moroccan music."

Karim looked up and smiled, never missing a note. His red traditional hat caught the light as he nodded in greeting.

4

A young girl in a bright caftan darted past, silver earrings glinting. "Khadija!" called a woman in a hijab who followed more sedately, carrying a tray of delicate glasses.

"That is Mina, our wonderful maid, and her niece Khadija," Mustafa explained. "They will be doing henna designs for our female guests tonight."

"Henna!" Emma said with a smile.

A side door swung open, and a regal woman entered, silver bracelets jingling. Her dark eyes swept the room as she adjusted her embroidered headscarf.

"Ah, and here is Amira," Mustafa said. "She reads fortunes - very famous in Marrakesh."

"This is amazing," Emma breathed again, squeezing Daniel's arm. Her gaze drifted to the courtyard garden just visible through arched doorways, where a fountain burbled among orange trees.

"Let me show you to your room so you can freshen up," Mustafa said. "Then please, join us back here for a magical Moroccan evening."

Daniel picked up their bags, and even he seemed invigorated.

Emma hung the new green and gold caftan she'd bought in the market in the carved wooden armoire, admiring how the silk caught the evening light streaming through the tall windows of the French doors to her private balcony. The room took her breath away - from the ceiling with its intricate carved plasterwork to the stone floor covered in handwoven rugs. Even the bed was exotic, draped in embroidered silk with more geometric carved wood forming the headboard.

A knock at the connecting door made her smile. "Come in!"

Daniel stepped through, his hair damp from a quick shower. "This place is incredible. Have you seen the bathroom? The sink is hammered copper."

"Everything feels magical." Emma smoothed a wrinkle from a summer dress. "I wish we had more than two days."

"We could always extend our stay." Daniel leaned against one of the carved arches that framed the doorway between Emma's sitting area and bedroom.

"Don't tempt me." Emma's phone buzzed and she glanced at the screen. "Oh! A text from Bridget."

"Everything okay at the bakery?"

"Huh." She paused to read. "Sort of? Apparently someone," she looked up, stole the delivery van?" Emma shook her head. "Why would anyone want my bright pink delivery van? Bridget said she'll explain when we get back."

Daniel raised an eyebrow. "Sounds like quite a story."

"We'll have plenty of stories too." Emma pulled Daniel in for a hug, then gestured at their surroundings. "Paris, Venice, and now Morocco? No one's going to believe half of what we tell them."

"Not to mention your penchant for stumbling across murders."

"Not here," Emma said, holding up her hand to stop him. "We're only here for two days. No murders. We don't have time for anything that exciting."

Daniel laughed and kissed the top of her head. "That's my Emma. Ready to head down? I think I hear Karim's music."

Emma slipped her feet back into her sandals. "Just let me grab my phone. I can't wait to see this Moroccan evening."

Emma followed Daniel down the winding stone staircase, the sound of Karim's *oud* growing louder with each step.

The hotel owner guided them to their seats at a low brass table inlaid with intricate patterns. Emma sank into the plush cushions, taking in the rich scents of spices and fresh bread wafting from the kitchen. Other guests were seated at nearby tables and Emma turned to the two men at the table beside theirs.

"Dr. James Grant," the silver-haired man introduced himself. "From the embassy in Rabat." He held out his hand.

"Daniel Lindberg," Daniel said. "And this is my girlfriend, Emma Harper. Rabat, eh? Getting some time away from the office?"

Dr. Grant smiled but Emma saw his shoulders tense. "It's always good to have a change of scenery."

Daniel nodded. "I know I'm happy to get away for a while, that's for sure. We're from Minnesota. Where are you from originally?"

Dr. Grant's eyes lit up. "Minnesota? My grandfather's from Minneapolis."

Emma smiled. "We won't hold that against you. We're from St. Paul. How is it working at the embassy?"

Dr. Grant grinned. "Yes, rival twin cities. As for the embassy, well, things have been... rather stressful lately. It's nice to get away."

The second man sat across from Dr. Grant, partially hidden behind a potted palm tree. Now, he cleared his throat. "Victor Novikov," he said in accented English. As a woman across the room laughed, Victor shifted in his seat.

"Emma," Emma said, holding out her hand. "Where are you from, Victor?"

"I am from Russia. Here to write a short piece on Arab culture."

Servers brought out baskets of round flat loaves of bread and steaming bowls of harira soup, its rich tomato and lentil aroma making Emma's mouth water. She tore off a piece of warm bread and dipped it in the fragrant broth.

"The eggplant salad is exceptional," Victor said, motioning to the vegetables arranged artfully on a painted platter. "But my favorite dish here is the stretchy pancake things they make in the morning. I hope you enjoy the breakfast. This hotel is a treat for me. I usually stay at more budget friendly places. But the food here." he raised his eyebrows. "It's the best."

"Won't you be here for breakfast?" Emma asked.

Victor shook his head. "No. I leave tonight for the Sahara."

Emma leaned forward, intrigued. "The Sahara? That sounds amazing. What part are you visiting?"

"Merzouga," Victor said, his pale green eyes lighting up. "The dunes there are magnificent, or so I'm told. I'll be meeting with some Bedouin families."

Daniel set down his spoon. "How long will you be out there?"

"Just one day." Victor dabbed his mouth with a napkin. "My guide will pick me up tonight. We'll drive through the night to catch the sunrise over the dunes. Then I'll spend the day interviewing locals about their traditions, their music, their relationship with the desert." He gestured to where Karim played in the corner. "Much like our friend here with his *oud* - the desert has its own traditions."

Emma noticed that Victor's shoulders rose as he spoke about his work. She guessed it was stressful for him, although to her it sounded magical. "What magazine do you write for?"

"Several freelance pieces," Victor said with a dismissive wave of his hand. "This one is for a travel magazine based in Moscow. They want an authentic perspective on desert life - not just the tourist experience of camel rides and camping." He reached for his water glass.

"Too bad it's just one day," Emma said.

Victor nodded. "I am a quick study, as you Americans say. One day is all I'll need to capture the essence of a place."

Emma raised her eyebrows, wondering if this could be true.

Dr. Grant cleared his throat. "The desert can be dangerous, even for a short trip. Have you arranged for proper supplies?"

"Of course." Victor's smile didn't quite reach his eyes. "My guide is very experienced. We'll have plenty of water, emergency equipment. It's all very well planned."

Emma sampled the salad, the blend of garlic and spices dancing on her tongue as Karim's music swelled. His fingers flew across the strings, eyes closed as he played a mesmerizing melody.

Laughter drew Emma's attention to the larger group seated at the table to their left as a woman in a flowing caftan settled onto the cushions.

"Adeline!" A dark-haired woman in an expensive-looking dress embraced a woman dressed in Moroccan clothes, but with red hair and freckles. "I'm so glad you made it."

Emma caught Daniel's eye, and he smiled. They both loved people watching.

An older man at the table saw them watching and reached across to shake hands. "I'm Brian Johnson," he said. "Fellow Americans?" When Emma and Daniel nodded, he said, "Wonderful. This is my daughter Ruby and her husband Derek." He gestured to the elegant woman and the well-dressed man beside her. "Ruby's friend Adeline just arrived from Fez, and this is my assistant for the Moroccan side of my business ventures, Fatima. I'm in the country on business."

Emma introduced herself and Daniel as servers brought out gleaming silver platters. The scent of cinnamon, chicken and saffron filled the air.

"The *b'stilla* is incredible," Fatima said, indicating the delicate phyllo pastry. "You must try it."

"Seven years ago we were celebrating our wedding in Paris," Derek said, reaching for Ruby's hand. But Ruby withdrew her hand to adjust a stunning, blood-red ruby necklace at her throat.

"And now we're in Marrakesh for your anniversary," Adeline said. "How lovely."

Ruby avoided her husband's attempt to take her hand again by serving herself from the lamb tagine. The dish was served in a peaked clay pot and smelled amazing.

"Are those prunes?" Emma asked, and Fatima nodded. "And sesame seeds. Dresia, the cook here, is amazing. And of course, the couscous!"

"So, you're here for business meetings?" Daniel asked, spooning couscous onto his plate.

Emma sampled the tender chicken tagine, the flavors of preserved lemon and olives melting on her tongue. Then the server brought the b'stilla to her table. Emma had never seen anything like it. She put the serving fork through the flakey layers and was amazed at the spiced poultry pie wrapped in phyllo dough and decorated with ground almonds, sugar, and cinnamon.

"Have I died and gone to food heaven?" Emma asked Daniel. "I have got to learn to make this!"

As servers carried away the main courses, the scent of honey and orange blossom wafted through the room as Khadija, the young girl, brought out platters of Moroccan pastries, their flower shapes glistening with honey and sesame seeds, and an assortment of almond cookies and fresh fruits.

"Where's my spoon?" An elderly woman across the room asked in a British accent as she patted the cushions around her. Her silver curls bounced as she searched, her red-framed glasses sliding down her nose. "I just had it a moment ago." She stood, searching, and then said to a server, "I'll need a new spoon, please. Mine has completely disappeared."

"Yes, madam," the server said. "But," he peered around her, "is that not your spoon? Beside your bowl?"

"Oh! So it is." The woman adjusted her glasses and laughed. "I'm so sorry. I've just returned from the most amazing expedition and I'm a bit tired! Three days in the Sahara with my childhood friend Margaret. But yes, I might be a little tired. And sore! Those camels!"

Emma nudged Daniel and nodded to the woman. Together they crossed the room to meet her. "Do you mind if we join you? I'm Emma Harper," Emma said. "And this is my friend, Daniel. Did you say you were in the Sahara?"

The woman set her newly found spoon down and held out a hand. "Edith Pimm, pleased to meet you both. Yes, camping under the stars! Though I must say, I'm rather looking forward to getting back to my cats and my quiet life in England tomorrow. My cat sitter sends daily updates, but Scarlet and Midnight do get anxious when I'm away."

The music swelled as Karim drew his fingers across the *oud* strings in an intricate melody and the room fell silent, mesmerized. When the song ended, spontaneous applause erupted from all the tables.

"It was good to meet you," Emma said. "Happy travels tomorrow!"

Back at their own table, Emma watched as Daniel picked up one of the almond cookies and bit into it. Her own eyes widened as she tasted one of the intricate, twisted pastries, its flower shape glistening with honey and sesame seeds.

"This is incredible," she said, reaching for her glass of mint tea. "What is this?"

"*Sh'bakia*," Fatima said. "A Moroccan specialty."

"I'm a baker, and I can usually guess what the ingredients are for something new, but I have never had anything like this!" She turned to Daniel. "I wish we were staying longer, so I could learn to make these."

"You're a baker?" Ruby, the stylish woman asked. "How wonderful!"

Mustafa stepped to the center of the room, his tall frame commanding attention. "My dear guests, tonight we have a special treat. Please welcome Amira El-Fassi, famous in Marrakesh for

14

her ability to see the future. Tonight, she will read your fortunes."

A woman in her sixties glided forward, her traditional Moroccan dress sweeping the floor. Silver-streaked black hair peeked from beneath an embroidered headscarf, and thick silver bracelets clinked at her wrists. Her dark eyes seemed to pierce through everyone she looked at.

"And here," Mustafa gestured to a young woman in a simple caftan and hijab, "is Mina, and her niece Khadija. They will create beautiful henna designs for any ladies who wish to have them."

"Henna?" Edith Pimm clutched her pearls. "You mean like tattoos?" Her eyes widened behind her red glasses. "What would my Mable and the others at the Women's Society say if I came back as a tattooed woman?" She let out a delighted laugh. "The scandal! Sign me up."

Khadija stepped forward shyly. "The henna is not permanent, madam," she said in a soft voice. "It will fade in two weeks."

"Oh! Well by that time Mable's shock will have worn off to." Edith said with satisfaction.

Emma's heart raced with excitement. Here she was, in a beautiful Moroccan hotel, about to experience fortune telling and henna painting. She couldn't believe her luck - this was exactly the kind of authentic experience she'd hoped to find in Marrakesh.

Emma settled into a cushioned chair as Mina began applying henna to her hands.

"Amira said I have wonderful surprises in my future," Emma said, smiling at Daniel.

He nodded. "I think she's right!"

Mina held Emma's hand. The intricate design flowed from the tip of the cone filled with dark paste, creating delicate swirls across the back of Emma's hand.

Behind the carved wooden screen where Amira was telling fortunes, Emma heard Edith's delighted gasp followed by laughter. The older woman emerged, her cheeks flushed.

"Oh, how marvelous! She said I'll take another grand adventure before the year is out. Isn't this fun? I think I might go to Tibet next!"

Daniel squeezed Emma's shoulder. "My turn. Let's see what the future holds!"

"Don't let her tell you anything too shocking," Emma teased, careful not to move her hands as Mina worked.

When Daniel returned he looked happy but refused to tell Emma what the older woman had told him. "It's a surprise," was all he would say before sipping more mint tea.

Adeline went next, her flowing caftan rustling as she disappeared behind the screen. The fortune-telling area was close enough that Emma caught snippets of Amira's melodious voice, though she couldn't make out the words.

"These flowers mean love and prosperity," Khadija explained, as Mina added petals to the design on Emma's wrist.

Ruby stood when Adeline returned. Her ruby necklace- so apt for her name- caught the lamplight as she walked to the screen turning blood red.

Khadija began moving the supplies to Adeline's table as Mina added the finishing touches to Emma's henna.

Minutes ticked by and conversation quieted as Mina applied henna to Adeline's hands. Ruby had been with Amira quite a while, and unlike with the other guests, Emma could no longer hear Amira's voice from behind the screen.

When Ruby finally emerged, her face was so white Emma was startled as she watched the elegant woman her make her way back to her seat between Derek and Brian.

"What did she say?" Adeline leaned forward.

"She-" Ruby's voice shook. "She said I'm in terrible danger. That death walks close behind me."

Derek let out a sharp laugh. "Come on, Ruby. You can't take this seriously."

"But she knew things," Ruby whispered. "Things she couldn't possibly know."

Victor rose quietly from his chair. He nodded a polite goodbye to Dr. Grant and slipped toward the door, his departure as unremarkable as his presence had been all evening.

Ruby whispered something Emma didn't catch, and Derek rolled his eyes. "Fortune tellers are all the same. They watch you all evening, learn a few things to impress you, and then tell you something dramatic to get more money out of you."

"You weren't there," Ruby snapped. "You didn't hear what she said about-" She cut herself off, glancing around at the other guests who had fallen silent. She lowered her eyes and said, "I'm not discussing this here."

Ruby's fingers trembling as she lifted her glass, spilling drops of mint tea onto the embroidered tablecloth.

Derek waved at one of the servers. "Another bottle of that Moroccan red." He turned to Dr. Grant. "Have you tried it? Excellent vintage."

Brian, Ruby's father, leaned forward with a forced smile. "Let's focus on having a pleasant evening. Ruby, remember that view from the Atlas Mountains I was telling you about? Fatima knows the perfect spot for a picnic."

Fatima nodded, her bangles catching the lamplight. "The wildflowers are beautiful this time of year. And the air is so clear you can see for miles."

"That sounds lovely," Ruby said, but her voice was hollow as she glanced at Derek.

Derek topped off everyone's wine glasses, pointedly skipping Ruby's. "To Moroccan hospitality," he declared.

Mustafa called the men to gather around a low brass table where he demonstrated the traditional tea-pouring technique. Emma watched, fascinated, as he lifted the silver teapot high above the glasses, creating a perfect stream of liquid that sparkled in the lamplight.

"The height creates tiny bubbles," Mustafa explained. "It makes the tea taste better and shows respect for your guests."

Daniel attempted the pour, tea splashing onto the table. Brian's try wasn't much better, but Derek managed a decent stream despite his unsteady hands.

Dr. Grant sat up taller, his movements precise. The tea arced gracefully into the glass, creating a crown of foam.

"Bravo!" Edith clapped, careful of her drying henna. The others joined in the applause.

"I'd try," Emma said, "but I don't want to ruin Mina's beautiful work."

The rich aromas from dinner still lingered, and Emma's curiosity got the better of her. "Could I meet the cook? The *b'stilla* was incredible."

Mustafa beamed. "Of course!" He walked to the kitchen door. "Dresia!" Then he shouted a stream of Arabic words Emma couldn't understand.

Dresia emerged from the kitchen, her traditional dress pristine despite what must have been hours of cooking.

Emma's eyes lit up. "Could you teach me to make the *b'stilla*? And those honey-soaked pastries-sh'bakia, I think they are called?"

Khadija translated rapidly, and Dresia's warm laugh filled the room as she responded in Arabic.

"She says she would love to teach you," Khadija explained. "But proper Moroccan cooking takes time to learn. The b'stilla alone needs days to make properly."

Emma's shoulders dropped. "Multiple days for one dish. Wow! I wish I could stay longer. But we leave in two days."

"Perhaps you could learn some Arabic instead?" Edith suggested. "I've picked up a few words. '*Ajee*' means 'come here' and '*S'lema*' means both hello and goodbye."

Emma tried the words, stumbling slightly over the unfamiliar sounds. Mina, Dresia, and Mustafa broke into encouraging applause.

"Not bad for a first try," Mustafa said with a warm smile, and Khadija grinned shyly as she nodded at Emma.

Chapter 2

Emma's sandals whispered against the stone tiles as she and Daniel made their way toward the stairs. The evening's festivities had wound down, leaving only the faint echo of Karim's music in her memory and the delicate henna patterns drying on her hands.

Ruby appeared from around the corner, her face still pale as she made her way beside them toward the stairs. "So," she asked, "what brings you two to Morocco?"

"We're on a summer trip through Europe," Emma said. "And we decided to take a quick detour down to Morocco on our way home. I have to admit, getting to experience a traditional Moroccan evening like this was worth the whole detour."

Ruby smiled and nodded. "It was something. What do you do back home?"

"I own a bakery in Minnesota."

"Minnesota! That's quite a change from here." Ruby gave a small laugh and Emma thought she was doing a wonderful job of small talk despite her obvious continuing distress, though whether it was more from the fortune or her husband's treatment of her, Emma wasn't sure. Ruby's gaze shifted to Daniel. "And you?"

"I'm with the police department." Daniel's voice carried that quiet authority Emma knew so well.

Ruby's eyes widened. "A policeman?"

"Detective, actually."

"A detective?" Ruby's fingers went to her necklace. "I... that's fascinating. Have you worked many interesting cases?"

"A few." Daniel nodded. "Though Emma here is getting to quite the little detective herself."

Emma felt her cheeks warm at Daniel's praise. She waved her hand, careful not to smudge the henna. "Oh, it's nothing like that."

"Nothing?" Daniel's eyebrows shot up. "You solved the murder at your bakery. And there was that case in Paris. And let's not forget Venice with the-"

"Daniel." Emma nudged him with her elbow, but he just grinned.

"Really?" Ruby's dark eyes sparked with interest. "You've actually solved murders?"

"I just happened to be in the right place at the wrong time." Emma shrugged. "Or wrong place at the right time. I'm never quite sure which."

"She's being modest," Daniel said. "Emma has a talent for putting pieces together. She notices things other people miss."

Ruby's fingers traced the gems at her throat again, her eyes distant. "That must be... useful. Being able to figure things out like that. Her gaze darted around the hallway before settling back on Emma's face.

There was something more she wanted to say - Emma was certain of it. "I just pay attention," Emma said softly. "Sometimes that's all it takes."

Ruby glanced again around the empty hallway. "Would you... would you both mind if we talked for a moment?"

Emma saw Daniel's nod and answered. "Of course."

Ruby led them to a small alcove off the main corridor where cushioned benches lined the walls beneath an intricately carved window. The streetlights outside cast patterned shadows through the glass.

"It's about my fortune." Ruby's hands trembled as she smoothed her silk dress. "You probably think I'm being silly." When Emma shook her head, Ruby gave her a sad smile. "What Amira said - it wasn't just vague warnings. She knew things. Private things."

Emma settled onto one of the benches. "What kind of things?"

With a deep breath, Ruby said, "She knew about the note." Her voice dropped to barely above a whisper. "She mentioned a threatening note I received last week. But I haven't told anyone about it. Not even Derek."

Daniel's posture straightened "What note?"

Ruby reached into her designer purse and withdrew a folded piece of paper, her diamond ring catching the light. "This arrived in my room, slipped under the door two days ago. I was the only one there." She held it out with unsteady fingers. "I've been carrying it with me ever since, trying to decide what to do."

Emma leaned forward as Ruby unfolded the paper. A crude message had been assembled from newspaper clippings. Her breath caught as she read, "YOU ARE VERY DEAD." The letters were uneven, cut from different fonts, creating a jarring visual against the white paper.

Ruby's hands shook as she refolded the note and tucked it back inside her purse. "Can you help me? Both of you? You're a detective, and Emma, you've solved murders. Please."

Daniel shook his head. "This is serious, Ruby. This happened here? In this hotel?" When Ruby nodded, Daniel said, "You need to report this to the local police."

"No, please." Ruby's perfectly manicured hands twisted together. "I don't want to involve the authorities. And please don't tell Derek or Daddy."

Emma frowned. "But, they should know about this."

"Derek would just laugh at me, like he did with the fortune. Like he does with everything I'm worried about. And Daddy..." Ruby's voice trailed off. "He'd probably cut the vacation short and whisk
24

me back to the States. I don't want to make things complicated."

"Ruby," Emma said, keeping her voice gentle. "You're not the one making this complicated. Someone is threatening your life - that's what's complicated here. Not you."

"But we're here for our anniversary trip. Just a few more days." Ruby's eyes glistened. "We can handle this quietly, you two and me. Figure out who's doing this without involving everyone. We don't need to make a big deal out of this, right?"

Daniel shook his head. "A death threat already is a big deal. And you say Amira, the fortune teller, knew about this?" He looked down at the paper. "This isn't the kind of thing to be investigated privately. You need to go to the authorities."

"Please." Ruby's voice cracked. "At least think about it? I don't know who else to turn to."

Emma exchanged a look with Daniel. She understood Ruby's fear, but Daniel was right - this was far more serious than a private investigation.

"I'm sorry," Emma said quietly. "Will you tell the police about this tomorrow morning, or should Daniel and I tell them?"

Ruby snapped her purse closed, her hands shaking. "I'll tell them," she whispered. "I'm sorry I bothered you." She stood, her eyes not meeting theirs. "Good night."

Emma watched Ruby disappear up the stairs, her heels clicking against the stone tiles.

Daniel pulled her close. "We did the right thing." His lips brushed her forehead. "Someone needs to investigate."

"I know." Emma leaned into him for a moment. Then, she pulled his forehead to touch hers. "Thank you for being someone who does the right thing."

They held hands as they headed up the stairs. At the top, they stood beside the railing to the open courtyard below and looked up at the half-moon.

"This is incredible," Emma whispered. "I can't believe we get to be here. Wasn't this evening amazing?"

Daniel gave a small laugh, his eyes on hers. "You can say that again. Wow. There was this beautiful girl sitting right beside me all evening. She has the best laugh, and she's smart as a whip."

Emma smiled. "Really? Did you get her number?"

Daniel bent his head and closed his eyes as he whispered, "Oh yes." And then he kissed her.

After a moment, Emma said, "We should get to sleep. I want to see everything in this city tomorrow."

Daniel nodded and squeezed her hands before he headed to his room.

As Emma reached for her own door handle, voices drifted from around the corner.

"You can't keep doing this, Ruby." Fatima's voice was sharp. "Think about what you're risking."

"Don't lecture me about risks." Ruby's whisper carried a bitter edge. "You're hardly one to talk about making careful choices."

"That's different and you know it."

"Is it? At least I'm honest about who I am."

A door slammed, cutting off their argument. Emma stood frozen, her key halfway to the lock. Before she could process what she'd overheard, another door opened further down the hall. Derek emerged from a room separate from where Ruby had gone. He balanced an empty wine bottle between his fingers, setting it carefully outside his door.

His gaze met Emma's. "Evening." His words slurred slightly as he gave a small wave before disappearing back into his room.

Emma slipped into her own suite, her mind racing. Separate rooms on their anniversary trip. The threatening note. Ruby and Fatima's cryptic argument. Something was very wrong here, despite the beautiful Moorish arches and peaceful fountain sounds drifting up from the riad below.

She changed into her pajamas, but sleep felt far away as she replayed Ruby's fearful expression when she'd shown them that note. Maybe they should have agreed to help after all.

Chapter 3

The morning sun cast delicate shadows across the courtyard as Emma and Daniel made their way down to breakfast. The scent of fresh bread and oranges filled the air. Emma spread honey on a piece of warm, stretchy bread and savored the sweetness while Daniel finished his coffee.

"Again," Emma said, "I have no idea what this is that I'm eating. How can there be baked things I can't even identify?"

Daniel grinned at her. "Mysteries. You find them everywhere. Even in baking."

Khadija walked through the courtyard and Emma motioned to her, remembering the Moroccan word for come here. "*Ajee*, Khadija."

The young girl looked up, surprised. Then a smile spread across her face. "Yes, madam?"

"What do you call this?" Emma asked, motioning to the platter of warm stretchy bread.

"*Msemmen*," Khadija said.

Emma just stared. "I'm sorry, can you say it again?"

"*Msemmen*. It is delicious." Her cheeks flushed pink, and she ducked her head as she spoke.

Emma laughed and nodded. "It is. That's true. You said… ms-em-en?"

Khadija nodded and Emma pulled out her phone and made a note. "Thank you! I have so many things I want to learn to make."

Khadija grinned shyly before hurrying across the courtyard and disappearing into the kitchen.

After breakfast, Emma and Daniel stepped out into the bustling streets, following the flow of people toward Marrakesh's main attraction, the *Jemaa el-Fnaa* square. Crowds thickened as they approached, voices rising in a mix of Arabic, French, and dozens of other languages.

The square sprawled before them, a vast open space larger than any plaza Emma had seen in Europe. Waves of people moved through the expanse, flowing between clusters of activity. Snake charmers sat cross-legged on carpets, their cobras swaying to the sound of wooden flutes. Women in colorful caftans hurried past carrying baskets, men selling water from what appeared to be animal hides wore colorful, wide-brimmed hats decorated in pompoms, while tourists stopped to photograph everything in sight.

Emma's gaze swept across rows of market stalls selling pyramids of spices - saffron, cumin, and paprika in deep jewel tones. Fresh dates and nuts spilled from woven baskets. The aroma of grilled meat and fresh bread wafted from food vendors.

"This is incredible," Emma said, stepping closer to Daniel as a man leading a monkey on a rope passed by. "It's like stepping into another century."

In the center of the square, a circle of onlookers gathered around performers - acrobats flipping through the air, storytellers gesturing dramatically as they spoke in rapid Arabic, and musicians playing traditional instruments Emma didn't recognize.

The Atlas Mountains rose in the distance, their peaks barely visible through the morning haze. Terra cotta buildings rimmed the square, their walls weathered by sun and sand. Emma noticed intricate geometric patterns carved into archways and doorways, so different from the classical architecture they'd seen in Europe.

"Look at those juice carts," Daniel pointed to a row of vendors selling fresh-squeezed orange juice from brass carts polished to a mirror shine. Pyramids of oranges balanced precariously on top.

A group of women walked past, their hennaed hands carrying shopping bags. Emma glanced down at her own hands, where the designs from the night before had darkened to a deep rust color.

"Look!" Emma hurried forward to watch a cobra rise from its basket, swaying to the notes of a snake charmer's carved wooden flute. The man sat cross-legged on a carpet, his weathered face focused on the snake's dance.

Daniel's hand tightened on hers. "Maybe we should keep our distance from that one."

A monkey in a tiny vest scampered past them, returning to its trainer who offered it a treat. The trainer caught Emma's eye and grinned, beckoning them closer.

"Photo? Very friendly monkey."

Emma hesitated, but Daniel gave her a gentle nudge forward. "When in Morocco..."

The small monkey wore a red vest with gold trim and clutched a tiny tambourine. Its dark eyes studied Emma as she approached, head tilting to one side.

"His name Malik," the trainer said in accented English. "Very smart. Show tricks for beautiful lady."

The monkey scampered down from his perch and did a little spin, shaking his tambourine. Emma laughed as Malik bowed with a flourish.

"How long have you had him?" Emma asked.

The trainer beamed. "Five years. He is like my son." He pulled a date from his pocket and handed it to Malik, who pulled it apart with nimble fingers before eating it.

Emma reached for her phone, but the trainer shook his head. "First, Malik give lady kiss."

Before Emma could react, the monkey darted forward and planted a quick peck on her cheek. Daniel burst out laughing as Emma's hand flew to her face.

"Now photo," the trainer said, grinning. "Very good luck, kiss from Malik."

Emma posed beside the monkey while Daniel snapped several pictures. Malik stayed perfectly still, as if he'd done this thousands of times before.

"How much?" Daniel asked, reaching for his wallet.

The trainer named his price and Daniel handed over the dirham notes. As they walked away, Emma scrolled through the photos on her phone.

"I can't believe I just got kissed by a monkey," she said, touching her cheek again. "Wait until Bridget sees these pictures."

"Fresh orange juice?" A vendor called out in English, gesturing to pyramids of oranges stacked beside his cart.

"Oh yes, please." Emma watched as he squeezed oranges into two tall glasses.

The juice was cold and sweet. "This might be the best orange juice I've ever had," she said, taking another sip.

They left the square and wandered deeper into the medina, where brass lamps cast intricate patterns on the walls. Daniel stopped at a shop displaying dozens of hanging lanterns.

"I love that one." He pointed to a brass lamp with blue and amber glass.

"For you, my friend, an excellent price." The shopkeeper named his price. But Daniel shook his head and offered a lower one.

Emma watched as they went back and forth, each time getting closer to agreement. Finally, they shook hands.

"You're good at this," Emma said as they continued through the narrow streets.

"Look who's here." Daniel nodded toward a café where Ruby and Adeline sat at a small table, sharing cups of mint tea and a plate of dates.

Emma was about to call out and say hello, but she saw that Ruby's eyes were red, her fingers twisting her napkin. Adeline leaned forward, speaking in low tones.

"Looks like they don't want to be interrupted," Emma said as she and Daniel passed by, unnoticed by the two women.

The next shop they entered was stacked floor to ceiling with rugs. Emma's eyes were wide as she took in the variety of colors and textures.

The shopkeeper approached.

"*S'lema*," Emma said, proud to use her new word for hello.

His face lit up. "*Ah salam ou alaykoum!* You speak Arabic! Welcome, welcome! I am

Mohammed." He shook their hands, then placed his hand on his heart. "You look for a rug to take home?" When Emma nodded enthusiastically, he gestured for them to sit.

Emma and Daniel took seats on leather poufs while a young man brought mint tea. Emma was about to say what she was looking for, but before she could speak, the shop keeper unfurled a rug before them.

"Beautiful Berber rug." Then he unfurled another. "Red one." he unrolled another. "Or in white and brown."

Emma and Daniel watched in amazement as Mohammed unfurled dozens of rugs, one on top of another. "How will I keep all these straight?" Emma whispered, and Daniel shook his head in amazement.

"This one is kilim," Mohammed said as he unrolled a flat-weave rug in beautiful red and blue geometric patterns.

Emma gasped. "It's beautiful."

After showing her the patterns in the rug and explaining where it was made and how well it would stand up to years of wear, Mohammed named his price.

Emma laughed out loud. "I can't afford-"

But Mohammed interrupted her. "But for you, my friend Emma, I make you a special price." He made a lower offer.

Emma made a counteroffer, and Mohammed pressed his hand to his chest in mock horror, but his eyes twinkled.

They went back and forth until they reached a price that made them both smile. As Mohammed wrapped the rug in blue paper, Emma felt a glow of satisfaction. The rug was going to look beautiful in her bedroom back home. And she was getting the hang of this fascinating city.

They turned down a narrow alley where shopkeepers displayed bundles of dried herbs, spices, dried lizards, and mysterious ingredients in woven baskets.

"Look at all these plants." Emma pointed to bunches of dried flowers hanging from the ceiling of one shop.

An older woman in a blue caftan beckoned them inside. "Welcome, welcome. I am Zahra. You need medicine? Love potion?" Her eyes sparkled with humor.

Emma stepped into the tiny dim shop, fascinated by the rows of glass jars filled with powders and dried plants and shocked by a dried lizard. "What's in these?" She pointed to the jars.

"Many things. This is for headache." Zahra held up a jar of dried leaves. "This is for stomach." She gestured to another containing what looked like tree bark.

"And this?" Daniel pointed to a jar filled with something that glowed faintly purple in the shadows.

"Ah, that very special. For good luck." Zahra winked.

Movement outside caught Emma's attention. Through the shop's narrow doorway, she spotted Brian Johnson and Fatima walking together. At a narrow passage, Brian motioned for Fatima to go ahead, his hand lingering on her back as she passed him.

"Headed to a business meeting?" Daniel asked quietly.

Emma raised an eyebrow. Something about their body language made her wonder if there was more to it.

Zahra motioned to a collection of small cloth bags filled with dried flowers. "In Morocco, we have old magic. Not tricks with cards or rabbits in hats." She crushed a sprig of dried purple flowers between her fingers, releasing their sharp scent. "Our magic comes from Allah and the earth."

Emma leaned closer to examine the delicate purple flowers Zahra held. "What do these do?"

"Lavender for peace. But real magic needs more." Zahra's dark eyes fixed on Emma. "We use combinations. Special words. Timing with moon phases." She pulled down a jar of rust-colored powder. "Saffron for joy. Rue for protection."

Daniel picked up a twisted root. "And this?"

37

"Careful." Zahra plucked it from his hand. "That one powerful. Used wrong, brings bad dreams."

Emma and Daniel looked at each other. "Wow," Emma said. "This city really is ancient."

"Very ancient," Zahra said. "Can I get you some herbs today?"

Emma shook her head. "No thank you. But this is fascinating."

As she and Daniel made their way out of the traditional medicine area, they heard a man calling to them.

"Please, come see my gems," he called out in accented English. "Finest in all Marrakesh."

Emma and Daniel stepped into the tiny shop, smaller than Emma's closet at home, where display cases held trays of glittering stones.

"I am Hassan Mirza." The gem dealer bowed slightly. "These amethysts are from the Atlas Mountains. These vanadinite also from Morocco."

Emma leaned over a case containing deep red stones. "They're beautiful."

"For you," Hassan said, taking one of the amethysts from the case.

"*Shukran*," Emma attempted, trying out the Arabic word for thank you she'd heard others use.

Hassan's face lit up. "You speak Arabic!"

Emma laughed. "No. Only a few words."

"You are honorary Moroccan," Hassan said, and Emma beamed.

38

Emma dropped into bed exhausted that evening. Marrakesh was like nothing she'd even dreamed of, and her brain was exhausted from all the new sights and sounds and smells. She fell asleep to the sound of prayer call drifting over the city.

In the wee hours of the morning, a crash jolted Emma from sleep. She sat bolt upright, her heart hammering as she looked for the source of the sound.

Another crash, and her head turned to the wall. The sound had come from next door - Ruby's room.

Emma scrambled out of bed, her bare feet hitting the cool stone floor. She fumbled for her robe in the darkness.

She rushed into the hallway. "Ruby? Are you okay?"

Silence.

Emma banged on Ruby's door. "Ruby!"

The hallway light flickered brighter as Mustafa came running. He clutched a ring of keys.

"Allow me," he said, fitting a key into the lock.

The door swung open. Moonlight streamed through the broken glass in the French door windows to the patio, casting jagged shadows across the room. A breeze stirred the silk curtains.

"Oh no." Emma's hand flew to her mouth.

Ruby lay sprawled on the ornate carpet, her dark hair fanned out around her head. A silver tea service lay scattered beside her, pieces of the delicate set glinting in the moonlight. A puddle of mint tea spread across the floor, the sweet scent mingling with the night air.

"Ruby?" Emma fell to her knees and put out a hand to check for a pulse, but there was no need. She was clearly dead.

"Do not touch anything." Mustafa pulled Emma back and took out his phone. "I must call the police."

Emma couldn't tear her eyes from Ruby's still form. The ruby necklace she'd worn at dinner was gone. In its place, angry red marks marred her throat.

Footsteps pounded down the hall. Daniel appeared in the doorway. "Emma, are you-" He broke off as he took in the scene. "Oh no. Step back, Emma."

More doors opened along the hallway. Brian emerged from his room, rubbing his eyes. "What's all the commotion..."

His words died as he looked into Ruby's room. "Ruby?" His voice cracked. "Ruby!"

Daniel blocked the doorway with his arm. "I'm sorry. You need to stay back. Mustafa is calling the police."

"Ruby!" Brian struggled against Daniel's hold before seeming to collapse against the wall, his shoulders shaking.

Adeline appeared, wrapped in a silk robe. She gasped. "Oh my gosh, Ruby!"

Derek stumbled out of his room, his eyes bleary. "What happened?" When he looked in the room, he gasped and took several steps back.

Mustafa spoke rapid Arabic into his phone while Daniel secured the area. Emma hugged herself, shivering despite the warm night air. The broken window gaped like a wound in the darkness, and somewhere in the distance, a muezzin began the call to prayer.

Chapter 4

Emma's hands shook as Daniel closed her hotel room door behind them. She sank onto the edge of her bed, the mattress barely giving beneath her weight.

"We should have done something." Her voice cracked. "Ruby showed us that note and we just... did nothing."

Daniel ran his fingers through his disheveled hair. "I told her to go to the police."

"But we knew she wouldn't." Emma wrapped her arms around herself, her silk robe cool against her skin. "Did you see—"

"Don't think about that right now." Daniel interrupted as he paced the length of the room, his bare feet silent on the stone tiles.

"How can I not?" Emma stood and walked to the French doors to the balcony. "YOU ARE VERY DEAD. That clearly wasn't an empty threat. And Amira knew about the note?" Emma swept her hair back from her face. "How could she have known?"

"Someone must have told her."

"But who?" Emma put her hand on the glass of the French door, feeling the coolness against her hot palm. "Ruby said she hadn't told anyone else." Her brow furrowed. "You don't think Amira's a killer disguised as a fortune teller, do you?"

Daniel shook his head. "Highly unlikely. Maybe Derek knew? They're having problems - you saw them at dinner. And they had separate rooms."

Emma shook her head. "She said she hadn't told anyone else. And if Derek knew about the threat, why would he laugh when Ruby got scared during her fortune reading?"

"To cover up his involvement? Maybe he sent the note and told Amira."

"You didn't see his face when he looked in that room. He seemed genuinely shocked."

"People can fake shock."

"What about her father, Brian? Did you see how devastated he was?"

"His father's grief looked real enough to me." Daniel sat on the bed. "But we can't rule anyone out yet."

Emma pressed her palms against her eyes. "I keep thinking about what Ruby said about wanting to keep things uncomplicated. If we'd just helped her..."

"Em, stop. This isn't your fault."

"We're the ones she trusted with this. A detective and..." She waved her hand. "Whatever I am. Amateur sleuth?"

"You're a baker who happens to be very observant." Daniel took her hand. "And you're right. We should have pressed harder when she showed us the note. But dwelling on it won't help Ruby now."

Emma walked to where he sat and squeezed his fingers. "Did you notice Victor acting strange at dinner? Always trying to hide behind that palm tree?"

"He said he doesn't like groups," Daniel said. "I noticed. But Em," Daniel held out his hand to her. "We need to let the police handle this."

The sky outside Emma's window shifted from black to deep purple with the faintest hints of pink. Early morning, or fajr, prayer call was just beginning as police officers arrived. Their hushed voices and careful footsteps in the hallway drew her and Daniel from her room.

A Moroccan police officer stood in the center of the hall, his white hat tucked under his arm as he spoke with two assistants. The shorter of the two assistants jotted notes in a small leather-bound book.

"Ah, you must be the American woman staying next door." The officer's English carried a slight French accent. "I understand you discovered the body?"

Emma nodded. "Not exactly. I heard the crash and-" She swallowed hard. "When no one answered, Mustafa came and opened the door."

"And you are?"

"Emma Harper. This is Daniel Lindberg. He's a detective back home in Minnesota."

The officer's eyebrows rose. "A fellow detective? Excellent. Though I hope you understand this is a Moroccan investigation."

"Of course." Daniel shifted his weight. "But there's something you should know-"

"One moment." Benali turned to his assistants. "Mohammed, check the security cameras. And Mohammed, interview the staff who were working last night."

The two assistants nodded and headed off in different directions.

"They're both named Mohammed?" Emma asked.

"As am I. Detective Mohammed Benali." He held out his hand and shook Daniel's hand and then Emma's, touching his heart after each one. "I am pleased to meet you. My apologies that it is under such tragic circumstances. We will, of course, speak with you soon." He nodded and turned to Ruby's room.

Emma peered past Benali into the room. Morning light spilled through the broken French door, catching on shards of glass scattered across the floor and balcony. A silver tea service lay in pieces, dark stains from the spilled mint tea on the rug.

"Daniel," Emma whispered as she pointed to the glass on the balcony. "Most of the broken glass fell outside."

"Suggesting it was broken from inside the room," Daniel said.

"Perhaps." Benali sighed, apparently having overheard their whispered conversation. "I'm hoping this proves to be nothing more than a robbery gone wrong. The ruby necklace is missing, after all. International incidents create so much paperwork." Benali made a note. "And what time did you hear the crash?"

"Around three, I think." Emma glanced at Daniel. "The call to prayer hadn't started yet."

"And you saw nothing suspicious out your own window? No one on the balconies?"

"I didn't look," Emma admitted. "I went straight to Ruby's door."

Benali nodded and wrote something else in his notebook. "Please remain available for further questions. And..." He gave them both a stern look. "Let's keep any relevant information between us, yes? No need to upset the other guests more than necessary."

Emma nodded.

"Who had access to Mrs. Astor's room?" Benali asked.

Mustafa clasped his hands together. "Only our maid, Mina. She cleans the rooms each morning while guests are at breakfast."

"Mina Bouazizi?" Benali made another note. "And she would know the layout of the rooms? Where valuables might be kept?"

"Yes, but-" Mustafa's face fell. "Mina has worked here for years. She is trustworthy."

"Yet she would know where the valuables were." Benali's pen scratched across the paper. "And this is Kasim's daughter, yes? Her family's financial situation is... difficult, if I am not mistaken."

Emma's stomach clenched. The image of Mina's gentle movements as she applied henna designs the night before seemed at odds with Benali's implications. The young maid's quiet dignity, her careful attention to each guest - none of it fit with someone capable of murder.

"We must follow all leads," Benali said, closing his notebook with a snap.

Voices carried up from downstairs- Derek's voice if she was not mistaken. Her thoughts drifted to his behavior. The wine bottle in the hall, the separate rooms, the tension crackling between him and Ruby at dinner. Her mind replayed the sharp edge in his laugh when Ruby showed fear over her fortune.

"I'll be right back," Emma whispered to Daniel.

She made her way down the curved staircase, its brass railings cool under her palm. Voices drifted up from the salon. Emma paused in the shadows of the stairwell.

Derek sat perched on the edge of an ornate chair, his fingers white-knuckled around a glass of
48

mint tea. One of Benali's assistants stood nearby, notebook in hand.

"Of course we argued." Derek's voice carried a brittle edge. "What couple doesn't? But I loved her."

"You had separate rooms," the officer noted.

"Ruby insisted." Derek set his tea down with a sharp clink on a brass table. "Said she needed space to think. About us. About everything." His hand trembled as he ran it through his carefully styled hair. "I gave her everything she could want: money, trips, a boat, all of it. And still-" He broke off, jaw clenched.

"When did you last speak with your wife?"

"After dinner. She was upset about some fortune teller's prediction." Derek gave a sharp laugh. "Nonsense, I told her. But now? Maybe the old woman was right."

Emma pressed further into the shadows as Derek surged to his feet, pacing the intricate carpet. His expensive loafers seemed out of place against the traditional patterns.

"Are we finished?" Derek snapped. "I'm in shock. This doesn't seem like the time. And I'd like to contact our embassy, make arrangements-"

"Soon, Mr. Astor. I have a few more questions."

Emma slipped back up the stairs thinking about Derek's words. His agitation could be grief, or guilt, or both.

She stood in the hallway, watching the strange tableau of hotel guests in various states of dress. The sun was rising, and early morning light filtered through the carved window screens, creating dancing patterns on the tile floor.

Edith Pimm shuffled forward in her floral bathrobe and fuzzy pink slippers, her silver curls askew. "Has anyone seen Fatima? Surely she's not still sleeping."

Benali looked around. "Fatima?"

"Another guest," Edith said. "The only one I haven't seen up and about with this horrid business."

Brian Johnson's face tightened. "She must be sleeping," he muttered.

But Benali looked up the hall. "Which room is hers?"

Edith pointed to the door beside Brian's, and Benali knocked loudly.

As Benali knocked, Brian turned and disappeared down the hall without a word, the click of his door lock lost in the sound of Benali's knocking.

"Fatima left the hotel after midnight," Mustafa said as he came up the stairs, addressing Detective Benali. "I was at the front desk when she went out. She didn't say where she was going."

"Please," Benali said, motioning Mustafa toward Fatima's door. "Can you open it for me?"

Emma followed as Mustafa unlocked Fatima's door with his master key. The room opened into a pristine suite, apparently untouched since housekeeping's last visit. Emma could see the perfectly made bed with its decorative pillows still arranged in careful formation.

A laptop sat closed on the writing desk. A half-empty glass of water stood beside it, lipstick marks on the rim. On a small brass table stood a silver tea service and three small glasses. The closet doors hung open, revealing Fatima's purple and mauve tailored suits and dresses still hanging in neat rows.

Detective Benali circled the room, his keen eyes scanning every surface. He paused at the nightstand.

"The bed has not been slept in," Benali noted, running a hand over the crisp duvet. "And her belongings are still here."

Emma watched from the hall as he went into the bathroom and returned.

Benali turned to Mustafa. "You will contact me the moment she returns?"

"Of course, Detective." Mustafa nodded.

They filed out of the room, and Mustafa locked the door behind them.

Emma touched Benali's sleeve. "Detective? Could I speak with you privately?"

Benali nodded and followed Emma to a quiet corner near the stairwell. Daniel joined them.

51

"Last night, I overheard an argument between Ruby and Fatima," Emma said. "I couldn't make out the words, but their voices were raised."

"When was this?"

"Just after dinner. And there's something else." Emma glanced at Daniel. "Two nights ago, Ruby showed us a threatening note she'd received."

Daniel nodded. "Cut-out letters from newspapers. It said, 'You are very dead.'"

Benali's pen moved across his notebook. "Where is this note now?"

"I don't know," Emma said. "Ruby kept it. She put it in her purse."

"And you didn't think to mention this earlier?" Benali's mustache twitched.

"We were waiting for a private moment," Daniel explained. "Ruby didn't want anyone to know about it. She said she hadn't told her husband or her father."

Benali closed his notebook. "I will need to search her room and belongings for this note. Thank you for telling me."

The investigation continued with Benali and the two Mohammeds talking to each person individually as hotel staff began setting up breakfast in the salon. The scent of fresh bread and coffee drifted up the stairs, but Emma's appetite had vanished.

Still, she and Daniel made their way down to join the others. The atmosphere was somber, punctuated by subdued conversations and worried glances. Dr. Grant sat alone, staring into his cup as he stirred his coffee endlessly. Edith sipped orange juice. She had changed into a bright purple dress that somehow made her look more fragile than her bathrobe had. Brian and Adeline sat together at a table in the corner. Brian's hands were shaking as he poked at his eggs.

Derek was nowhere to be seen.

Mina and Khadija carried in plates of pastries, cups of yogurt, sliced fruit, and fresh squeezed orange juice. Emma picked at a piece of bread, thinking about Ruby and the note. Daniel sipped his juice and watched the other guests. To Emma's surprise, Amira, the fortune teller, was seated at a table against the far wall sipping tea and eating fruit. Did she work for the hotel, Emma wondered. She'd assumed Amira was just a local businesswoman. Emma wondered again about how Amira knew about Ruby's note.

Just as the staff began clearing away the nearly untouched breakfast dishes, footsteps echoed in the entrance. Emma looked up expecting to see the police or Fatima.

But Victor appeared in the doorway, dusty and smiling. He stopped short when he saw the somber faces.

"What has happened?"

Mustafa appeared and took Victor's arm, guiding him back out of the dining room. Emma heard a murmured conversation, and then Victor said loudly, "Dead? How?"

A couple of minutes later, Victor came back into the salon. He stared around at the other guests, then sank into an empty chair, dropping his traveling bag at his feet.

When Khadija offered him tea, he took it without appearing to notice what he was doing.

Everyone, it appeared, was in shock at Ruby's tragic death. Which left Emma wondering, *could* it have been a break-in gone wrong, like Benali hoped it was?

Chapter 5

Detective Benali strode into the salon, his blue uniform crisp and so out of place against the crumpled demeanor of the guests. He cleared his throat.

"Madams and Monsieurs, I must inform you that no one may leave Marrakesh until we complete our investigation."

"What?" Edith's spoon clattered against her plate. She patted a napkin over her flowing dress. "I can't miss my flight! My cats—" She looked up, exasperation written in every feature. "You're not serious, surely."

Emma watched as Benali's expression remained impassive despite Edith's distress. His mustache twitched slightly.

"Madame Pimm, I regret this inconvenience, but a woman is dead."

"But my cats—" Edith's voice quavered. "And besides, I couldn't possibly have killed anyone. I'm seventy-three years old!"

Amira's silver bracelets clinked as she adjusted her headscarf. "That is exactly what a murderer would say, no?"

Edith's mouth fell open. A startled laugh escaped her. "My word, you can't be serious?" Her gaze darted around the room, seeking support.

Brian said quietly, "My daughter is dead, and it's possible that someone in this room killed her."

His hands were shaking as he reached for his glass. The morning sun caught the dark circles under his eyes.

"Well," Edith said. "That's true. I'm as shocked as anyone. And I'm sorry, Mr. Johnson. Truly." She dug through her oversized purse. "My flight leaves this evening. I assume you'll pay for the ticket change? And for my cat's extended care? My neighbor who is watching them only has enough food to feed them through Thursday." There was a pause as everyone watched her. "Where is my ticket? I had it right here..."

"Your cats' care?" Benali's eyebrows rose. "Madame, as Mr. Johnson said, a woman is dead."

"Which is precisely why you should be looking for Fatima instead of keeping us here." Edith's red glasses flashed as she gestured. "She vanishes the same night Ruby dies? That can't be coincidence."

Brian pushed back from his table, chair legs scraping against tile. "Fatima would never hurt Ruby. They were the best of friends."

Adeline rolled her eyes behind Brain's back and Emma's stomach tightened as she remembered the argument she'd overheard between the two women.

"Excuse me, Detective," Victor said tentatively. "I have a flight to Moscow tonight." Victor brushed desert dust from his pants and motioned to his travel bag. "I was not even here when this happened."

"You maintained your room, yes?" Benali asked.

"Well, yes, but—"

"Then you stay." Benali's tone left no room for argument.

Victor shook his head. "That is not possible. I'm sorry. This trip has cost too much already. I fear the story I'm writing won't cover these extra expenses."

Emma watched him with interest. For someone claiming money troubles, keeping an expensive hotel room while away seemed odd.

"I understand this is inconvenient," Benali said to the room at large. "But until we determine what happened to Mrs. Astor, everyone must remain available for questioning."

"But my cats—" Edith began.

"Perhaps you can arrange for your neighbor to pick up additional food," Benali offered.

Edith subsided.

Brian rubbed his face, exhaustion evident in every line of his body. "How long will this take? When will we know what happened?"

"As long as necessary," Benali replied. He surveyed the room once more before departing, boots clicking against the tile floor.

Emma watched the various reactions around her. Dr. Grant hadn't said a word and appeared lost in thought. Mina and Khadija moved quietly to collect his dishes. Victor stared around at the other guests and accepted a cup of coffee. Edith continued searching her purse, lips moving as she whispered to herself. Amira appeared calm, even almost cheerful. Adeline's eyes were red and her breakfast, Emma saw, was untouched. And Brian... Brian just looked lost.

A couple of hours later, after a long shower and time clearing her head, Emma sank onto one of the benches in the hotel's garden, her head spinning with the morning's events. Daniel pulled up a chair beside her, his phone already in hand.

"I'll call the airline," he said. "But I'm not sure how many days we should add."

Dr. Grant paced near the fountain, slightly disheveled. "This is a disaster. I have meetings scheduled all next week."

"Can't you reschedule them?" Emma asked.

"It's not that simple." He ran a hand through his silver hair. "Things have been... tense at the embassy lately. With the ambassador. I've already used most of my leave for the year, and I need to save what's left for Thanksgiving."

"Thanksgiving?" Daniel looked up from his phone.

"My sister's expecting her first child. The whole family's gathering in Boston." Dr. Grant's shoulders slumped. "I promised I'd be there. This was supposed to be a quick trip, just a couple of days." He shook his head.

Amira floated through the garden on her way to the front entry, her silver bracelets catching the morning light. "The police will take as long as they need. Death does not bow to our schedules."

Emma had learned from Khadija after breakfast that Amira often stayed at the hotel, taking advantage of her friendship with Mina to avoid the long journey home.

"But I just live in Rabat. They can reach me there. And what about diplomatic immunity?" Dr. Grant protested.

Amira replied simply, "The truth must be found."

Daniel touched Emma's arm. "The airline has flights on Friday, but there's nothing available for two weeks after that."

Emma's stomach churned. "Two weeks? But the bakery—"

"I know." Daniel squeezed her hand. "Maybe we should book the flights for Friday? We can always change them again if we need to."

Dr. Grant stopped pacing. "Friday might be cutting it too close. Officer Benali doesn't strike me as someone who rushes anything. Do you know the phrase *Ensha' Allah*?"

Emma and Daniel shook their heads, and Dr. Grant gave a wry smile. "You will."

Amira turned before the exit. "It means "If God is willing." Which is how we live in Morocco. Things happen in God's time, not on our schedule."

Daniel raised his eyebrows. "So, maybe not Friday?"

Dr. Grant gave another wry smile. "I'd bet against it."

Emma stifled a yawn. The lack of sleep was catching up with her. "I need to rest. I can't think straight anymore."

"Go," Daniel said. "I'll handle the flight changes."

Emma stood, her legs heavy with exhaustion. As she headed for the stairs, she heard Dr. Grant say something about the ambassador leave requests. Amira drifted out the front door and into the narrow alley.

The morning sun streamed through the ornate windows, casting intricate shadows on the stone tiled floors as she made her way up to her room. Despite her exhaustion, Emma couldn't help but notice how beautiful the hotel was in the morning light.

At the top of the stairs, Emma paused outside Ruby's room. There was no police tape, but the door was firmly shut. She stared at it, wondering what had happened. Who had done this? Without noticing, she moved closer to the door, her hand hovered above the door handle. Was it interfering if she looked around? She glanced at the empty hallway. It wasn't a problem if she didn't disturb anything, she reasoned as she pushed handle down. The hinges creaked in the morning quiet.

The room felt different like a crime scene. Despite the sunlight that streamed through the side window, highlighting dust motes dancing in the air, it felt as if tension was etched into the walls. The sheet that had been taped up to cover the broken French door fluttered in the breeze, creating shifting shadows across the intricate patterns of the Moroccan rug.

Emma's gaze fell to the dark stain where the mint tea had spilled. Shards of glass from the broken tea set still littered the floor, catching the light. The police had marked several pieces with small, numbered tags.

"I really should go to bed," Emma whispered to herself, but her feet carried her further into the room.

The air still held traces of Ruby's perfume mixed with the lingering scent of mint. Emma's throat tightened as she remembered Ruby's pleadings as she showed them the threatening note just a day or so ago. If only they'd done something, rather than waiting for her to tell the police about it.

A glint of color near the floor caught her eye. Emma crouched down, careful to avoid the glass fragments. Among the broken pieces lay part of a tea glass, its delicate pattern still intact despite the fall. But what drew her attention was the mark on its rim – a distinct lip print in a muted shade of lipstick.

"That's strange." Emma tilted her head, studying the color. The mauve tone seemed at odds with Ruby's bold style. She'd noticed Ruby's signature red lipstick the night before – a bright, confident shade that matched her namesake necklace.

Emma rocked back on her heels, frowning at the discovery. Someone else had drunk from that glass. But who? And when?

Her eyes burned with exhaustion, and she swayed slightly as she stood. The questions would have to wait. She needed sleep before she could make sense of anything else.

Chapter 6

Emma made her way into the salon. Her nap had helped, but her mind still felt foggy. Daniel told her he'd switched their tickets to Friday on the off chance the investigation was done by then.

Emma nodded and her face brightened as she turned to Dresia, who was arranging fresh flowers on one of the side tables.

"That breakfast yesterday – the stretchy pancakes. What was it called again?"

Dresia's face brightened. "*Msemmen*. You like?"

"It was amazing. And if we're here an extra couple of days I'd love to learn-" But Emma stopped as a booming voice from across the salon interrupted her.

"How dare you keep this from us?" Brian Johnson stormed across the salon, his face flushed with anger. Adeline trailed behind him, her green eyes rimmed in red.

Emma's stared as Brian planted both his hands on their table. "My daughter showed you a threatening note, and you didn't tell me? You just… did nothing?"

Daniel straightened in his chair. "Mr. Johnson-"

"Benali just told us about it," Adeline cut in, her voice trembling. "Why would Ruby show a note like that to strangers instead of her own friends and family?"

"Because Daniel's a detective," Emma said, her voice smaller than she intended. "We were talking after dinner and-"

"A detective?" Brian's laugh was harsh. "Then you should have known better. My daughter might still be alive if you'd done something."

Emma's chest tightened. "Ruby specifically asked us not to tell anyone. She didn't want to cause trouble-"

"Cause trouble?" Adeline's scarf slipped down, revealing her auburn hair. "She's dead."

"I know," Emma said. "We told her she wasn't the one causing trouble."

"We told her to go to the police," Daniel said, his tone steady. "Or talk to her family."

"But," Brian shot back, "you knew she was in danger, and you let her handle it alone. You did nothing to protect her!"

Emma pushed back her chair and stood. "You're right. We should have done more. And we feel terrible about it. We're sorry."

"A bit late for that, isn't it?" Adeline snapped.

Emma glanced behind Adeline and Brian, noting Derek's absence from this confrontation. Shouldn't Ruby's husband be the one most upset about the note? But she kept the observation to herself as Brian and Adeline's accusations continued to rain down.

"We'll do whatever we can to help find Ruby's killer," Emma said firmly, though guilt gnawed at her insides.

Brian shook his head in disgust and turned away. Adeline lingered, her expression a mix of grief and anger. "Please do," she said as Detective Benali appeared in the doorway, a sheaf of papers in his hands.

"Madam Idrissi," he nodded to Adeline. "Ms. Harper. Detective."

Daniel stepped forward. "Detective, about our flights - I've extended them to Friday, but should we push them back further?"

Benali adjusted his white hat with the black brim. "*Ensha' Allah* we will know somethings soon. Look, I hope this might be a simple break-in gone wrong. If that's the case, we will find the thief who committed murder, and you could leave in a day or two."

"A break-in?" Daniel's tone was skeptical. "With that threatening note?"

Benali shrugged. "Perhaps they are unrelated. Street thieves can be opportunistic. The ruby necklace was valuable. I'm checking with the gem dealers in the city to see if anyone tries to sell it."

"That's smart," Daniel nodded. "But in my experience, coincidences are rare. Surely the note indicates this wasn't a simple break-in."

Benali looked unhappy at this, but did not reply.

"Would we be allowed to do some sightseeing while we wait? At least see more of Marrakesh?"

"Yes, of course. Just don't leave the city." Benali folded his papers and tucked his notebook into his pocket. "I need everyone available for follow-up questions."

Adeline stepped closer. "You'll find who did this, right?"

"We're pursuing every lead, madame," Benali assured her. "The gem network in Marrakesh is tight knit. If someone tries to fence that necklace, we'll know."

"Thank you," Adeline nodded. But as Benali made his way to the door, his footsteps echoing against the tile floor, she turned to Emma and Daniel and whispered, "Please help. Moroccans are wonderful. But they are not the fastest- I know. I am married to one. I don't think I can handle it if this drags out forever."

Emma gave her hand a squeeze. "We will." Then she stepped forward before Benali could leave. "Detective, what about the lipstick on the broken tea glass in Ruby's room?"

Benali paused, his hand on the door handle. "What lipstick?"

"On one of the broken glasses. It's a mauve color - not the bright red Ruby usually wore."

Benali's mustache twitched. "Ms. Harper, perhaps you should focus on enjoying the sights of Marrakesh. Leave the investigating to those trained for it."

"But-"

Benali's tone grew firmer. "A murder investigation is men's business. Professionals. Not professional bakers, madam. Detectives."

Heat rose in Emma's cheeks. "The lipstick wasn't Ruby's."

Benali glanced at Daniel, as if seeking male solidarity. "Detective Lindberg, surely you agree your companion would be happier visiting the gardens or shopping in the souks?"

"Actually," Daniel said, "Emma has an excellent eye for detail. She's helped solve several cases back home."

"Ah yes." Benali's laugh was dismissive. "Women are wonderful sources of gossip, no? They notice who speaks to whom, who wears what." He waved his hand. "But real detective work requires years of training."

Emma's jaw clenched. She opened her mouth to respond that noticing what people wear includes shades of lipstick, but Benali was already heading out the door.

"Don't worry about the lipstick, Ms. Harper," he called over his shoulder. "My team will handle everything."

Emma watched him leave, heat rising in her chest.

Adeline, however, was staring at Emma. "Good for you. And what do you mean, there was lipstick on one of the glasses? It wasn't Ruby's? Are you sure."

"It was mauve," Emma said quietly as her eyes lingered on the door Benali had left through. "And Ruby wore-"

"Bright red," Adeline finished.

Chapter 7

The following day, Emma settled into one of the low cushioned chairs in the hotel lobby, appreciating how the tall windows flooded the space with sunlight. The clear panes offered glimpses of the terracotta-colored walkway and a tiled wall outside. She checked her phone - 11:55. Adeline had promised to meet her at noon for shopping.

Mustafa stood behind the front desk, rubbing his temples as he sorted through a stack of papers. The usually cheerful hotel owner looked exhausted, dark circles shadowing his eyes.

"Long couple of days?" Emma asked.

Mustafa looked up. "Yes, very long. The police, they ask many questions. Over and over." He shuffled the papers with a weary sigh. "And now I must change everyone's reservations. And cancel reservations for people who were going to arrive today, as their rooms are still occupied."

Emma nodded. "That does sound exhausting. I'm sorry."

Mustafa gave her a small smile and said, "*Shukran.*" When Emma looked confused, he said, "It means *thank you* in my language."

"*Shukran,*" Emma said, trying out the word, and Mustafa nodded his approval. "I wanted to ask

you something about the night Ruby died." Emma
said. "You said Fatima left late?"

"Yes, around one in the morning." Mustafa's
shoulders slumped. "She came down those stairs."
He pointed to the curved staircase. "She seemed...
how do you say... agitated?"

"Did she have any bags with her?"

"No, just her purse. The small black one she
always carries." He spread his hands. "I thought she
would return quickly. She said nothing about where
she was going."

"You've told Detective Benali all this?"

"Of course. First thing." Mustafa
straightened the guest register. "But still he asks
again and again."

The front door opened, and Amira glided in,
her silver bracelets catching the sunlight, her
henna'd hands wrinkled. She nodded to Emma
before disappearing down the hallway toward the
salon.

Emma's gaze followed her, and through the
arched doorway where she spotted Derek slouched
in a chair, a half-empty wine bottle on the table
beside him. Even from this distance, she could see
his hand trembling as he lifted his glass.

The sound of footsteps on the stairs drew her
attention. "Emma!" Adeline called out. "Sorry to
keep you waiting. Ready to brave the souks?"

Emma followed Adeline through the winding alleys of the medina, marveling at how her new friend navigated the maze-like passages with such confidence. The afternoon sun cast shadows through the latticed coverings stretched between buildings overhead.

Adeline, who lived in Fez and was married to a Moroccan man named Mohammed- like Benali and his assistants- appeared to know her way around Marrakesh and to be fluent in Arabic.

"Watch out!" Adeline pulled Emma aside as a donkey plodded past, laden with an improbable cargo - a flat-screen TV balanced in woven baskets across its back.

"Ok!" Emma laughed. "That's not something you see every day."

"Oh, you'd be surprised." Adeline smiled. "I've seen everything from washing machines to refrigerators transported by donkey through these alleys. Fez is even older than Marrakesh, and the city is a beautiful ancient labyrinth."

They passed a tiled fountain where women gathered with water vessels, their voices echoing off the walls as children played nearby with a soccer ball.

"The fabric souk is just ahead." Adeline gestured toward an archway draped overhead with flowing textiles. "Isn't it stunning?"

Emma looked up at the fabrics draped overhead, entranced. "It's like a scene from a fairy

71

tale. How long have you known Ruby? Did I hear that you went to school together?"

"Yes, in Switzerland." Adeline's voice softened. "She was incredibly fun back then. Before Derek."

They stepped into a tiny shop barely wider than Emma's arms could stretch. Shelves of folded silks and other fabrics reached to the ceiling in brilliant jewel tones. Emma selected a caftan to try on and slipped it over her jeans and shirt as they talked.

"Derek seems..." Emma paused, searching for the right word.

"Controlling? Cold?" Adeline ran her fingers along a bolt of emerald silk. "I never liked him. Ruby deserved better than someone who treated her like a possession."

"What do you mean?"

"Those jewelry gifts- the necklaces and the rings- weren't about love. They were about ownership. He didn't want her to travel without him. Or to have any of her own ideas. I'd been encouraging her to leave him."

Emma paid for the caftan. A spice merchant's cart rolled past the shop, filling the air with the scent of cinnamon and cumin as Emma followed Adeline deeper into the textile district, where they emerged into an open courtyard lined with rug shops.

"I'd love to find a small prayer rug," Emma said.

"*Ajee*." Adeline said as she motioned for Emma to follow her into a shop where rugs hung and were stacked on every surface. Quietly she whispered, "Let me help you bargain."

As had happened when Emma and Daniel looked at rugs, this shop keeper began unrolling rugs of all sizes and colors.

"I'd like a prayer rug," Emma said. "Maybe in blues?"

When the man had unrolled dozens of rugs, Emma shook her head. "They're all so beautiful! Can I see those three again, maybe next to each other?"

When she had chosen one she loved, Emma watched in amazement as Adeline haggled in rapid-fire Arabic with the merchant, their animated discussion punctuated by scowls and dramatic gestures. Finally, Adeline turned to her with a triumphant smile.

"He'll take four hundred dirhams."

"Is that good?"

"Very. He started at twelve hundred."

The shopkeeper also appeared pleased as he bid Emma and Adeline good-bye and urged them to return again.

With her new rug tucked under her arm, Emma followed Adeline back into the narrow streets and alleys. They walked into the jewelry district, and Emma up ahead, caught a glimpse of a familiar blue jacket and dashingly handsome man disappearing into a shop.

"Daniel!" she called out, a grin spreading across her face. But her voice was lost in the bustle of the marketplace. By the time they reached the tiny gem shop, Daniel was nowhere to be seen.

"*Marhaba!*" The jolly gem dealer welcomed them, his bushy black beard nearly hiding his smile. "Please, my friends, come see my treasures."

Emma stepped back into the street to look for Daniel, but there was no sight of him. Wondering what he'd been doing there, she stepped back into the closet-sized space surrounded by shelves of gems and fossils.

"Hassan Mirza is my favorite gem dealer in Marrakesh," Adeline said. "He always gives me a good price."

Hassan beamed at this and motioned to his wares.

Emma studied the cases of glittering stones while Adeline chatted with Hassan in Arabic. A display of fossils caught her eye - ancient creatures preserved in stone with surprising detail.

"This trilobite is beautiful," Emma said, pointing to a perfectly preserved specimen. "It looks like something from a museum."

Adeline nodded. "Most fossil collections in museums include several fossils from Morocco."

"*Na'am*, yes. From the Atlas Mountains!" Hassan's eyes lit up. "Very old, very special." He lifted it down and Emma was surprised at its weight. "Shall I wrap it for you?"

Emma nodded, and as Hassan wrapped her purchase, Emma's mind turned to Daniel's visit to the gem shop. He must be following up on Ruby's missing necklace, just as Benali had mentioned, and as they'd promised Adeline they would do. She made a mental note to ask him about it later.

"Can I ask you something?" Emma said as Hassan handed her the fossil. "Has anyone come in to sell a ruby necklace?"

Hassan looked confused, and Adeline translated.

"No. *La*." The gem dealer shook his head. "The police ask the same thing. I have heard nothing of this."

"Thank you. *Shukran*."

Emma and Adeline emerged from the shop into an alley filled with the scent of fresh oranges and mint from a nearby produce stand. A group of children darted past, playing some kind of chasing game, and Emma's stomach growled. She hadn't realized how long they'd been shopping. It was almost dinner time.

"I love how alive everything is here," Emma said. "It's so different from back home."

"That's what drew me to Morocco in the first place," Adeline replied. "Every corner holds a new surprise."

They made their way back through the winding streets of the medina toward Hotel al Zuhur, their shopping bags bulging. The afternoon heat had faded, and the call to prayer echoed from nearby minarets.

"I can't wait to show Daniel the fossil," Emma said as they passed through the hotel's ornate entrance into the cool lobby. The familiar scent of orange blossoms from the courtyard garden greeted them.

Mustafa looked up from his desk. "Ah, welcome back! I hope you found some treasures in our souks?"

"*Shukran*," Emma replied, proud to use one of her newly learned Arabic words. She glanced around the lobby. "We did! Is Daniel back yet?"

Mustafa shook his head. "I have not seen Detective Lindberg since this morning."

That was odd. Emma had assumed Daniel would be back by now, especially after spotting him at the gem dealer's shop.

"I need to freshen up before dinner," Adeline said, adjusting her silk scarf over her hair. "These narrow streets are dusty."

Emma climbed the stairs to her room, her new purchases weighing heavily in her tired arms.

As she approached her door, she heard a muffled sob from inside.

She pushed the door open to find Mina on her knees, scrubbing the tile floor. Khadija stood nearby, holding clean towels. Tears streamed down Mina's face as she worked.

"Oh, Mina!" Emma set her bags down. "Are you alright?"

Mina startled at Emma's voice. She scrambled to her feet, nearly knocking over her bucket of cleaning water. "*Asfa, asfa,*" she repeated, backing away.

"No, please - it's okay." Emma reached out, but Mina darted past her into the hallway, leaving her cleaning supplies scattered across the floor.

Khadija bent to pick up the fallen cloths. "I am sorry," she said in her quiet, careful English. "My aunt, she is very worried."

"Because of the police?" Emma asked softly.

Khadija nodded, gathering the rest of the cleaning supplies. "Detective Benali asks many questions about my aunt. But she does not hurt anyone." The girl's brown eyes were earnest. "She needs this job. For her family. Her *baba* is not well."

Emma remembered Benali's suspicions - that as a maid, Mina would have known where Ruby kept her valuables. But watching Mina's niece carefully stack the fresh towels, Emma couldn't reconcile the image of the gentle maid with murder.

"Her father is sick?" Emma asked.

"Yes. And my other uncle, he hurt his arm in the farm machines. Cannot work." Khadija straightened the items on Emma's bedside table. "Aunt Mina takes care of everyone now."

Emma's heart ached. She'd seen how carefully and quietly Mina moved through the hotel, how meticulously she cleaned. This was not someone who would risk everything on a violent robbery, Emma felt sure of it.

"I wish I could tell her not to worry," Emma said.

Khadija gave her a small smile. "I will tell her. *Shukran*." She gathered the cleaning supplies and slipped out of the room, leaving Emma alone with her thoughts about the frightened maid and the glimpse of Daniel in the medina.

Emma settled onto one of the low cushioned seats in the hotel's salon, inhaling the aroma of spices wafting from the kitchen. The evening light filtered through the carved wooden screens, casting intricate patterns across the tile floor.

Edith Pimm was already seated nearby, peering through her bright red glasses at a menu. "I do hope they serve that wonderful soup again. What was it called? Harira?"

"Yes, the tomato and lentil soup," Dr. Grant confirmed from his spot across the room. He'd loosened his tie and looked more relaxed than he had earlier. "Did you know it's what Moroccans typically break their fast with during Ramadan?"

Victor sat alone at a small table, writing in a leather-bound notebook, working on his article, Emma assumed. His wire-rimmed glasses caught the light as he glanced up occasionally, observing the other guests.

Brian and Adeline occupied a table near the fountain, speaking in low voices. Derek sat apart from them, staring into his wine glass.

Khadija moved quietly between the tables, offering fresh bread from a woven basket. "*Khobz*," she said softly as she reached Emma's table. "Still warm."

The bread's yeasty scent made Emma's mouth water. "*Shukran*, Khadija."

Quick footsteps echoed in the hallway and Daniel appeared in the doorway. His clothes were dusty, but his eyes were bright. He crossed to Emma's table and gave her a kiss on the cheek.

"I need to grab a quick shower," he said. "Save me a seat?"

Emma lowered her voice. "Did you learn anything at the gem dealer's shop today?"

Daniel's smile faltered. "Gem dealer?"

"This afternoon, in the medina. I saw you there and called out to you. But you didn't hear me."

"I don't know what you mean." Daniel shifted his weight. "I wasn't anywhere near the gem dealers today."

"But I saw you." Emma frowned. "Where were you all day?"

Mina came in with a platter of couscous and vegetables, and Daniel looked up at her before answering.

"We can talk later. I should get cleaned up for dinner."

"If you're investigating something, I want to help," Emma whispered. "We're supposed to be working together on this."

"Right. I'll be right back down." Daniel squeezed her shoulder and headed for the stairs.

Emma watched him go, her earlier contentment evaporating. She was certain she'd seen him in the medina. What wasn't he telling her?

"Everything alright, dear?" Edith asked, peering at Emma over her glasses.

"Fine," Emma managed a smile. "Just tired from shopping."

Dr. Grant checked his watch for the third time in as many minutes. "I don't suppose anyone's heard from Benali? I really need to get back to Rabat."

"At least you work in Morocco," Victor said without looking up from his notebook. "My editor in Moscow is not pleased about my extended stay."

Derek let out a swear word and everyone looked at him in shock. "None of us planned to be here this long," he said sharply. He drained his wine glass and held it out as Khadija passed.

Emma looked at Daniel's empty seat as the sound of plates clinking in the kitchen and quiet conversation filled the salon. She kept replaying that moment in the medina - she was certain she'd seen Daniel. Hadn't she?

Chapter 8

The following morning, Emma stood in the hotel's kitchen and watched in fascination as Dresia's hands moved with practiced precision, layering the delicate phyllo dough with butter. The kitchen smelled of warm spices - cinnamon, saffron, and something else Emma couldn't quite identify.

"First, we cook pigeon with stock," Dresia explained as Khadija translated. "But we also can use chicken. More easy to find."

"The secret is in the spices," Khadija added with a shy smile. "We mix sweet and spices."

Emma nodded, carefully folding the paper-thin phyllo as Dresia had demonstrated. "In my bakery, we mostly keep sweet and savory separate."

"But this is Morocco." Dresia gestured expansively. "Here, we know life is both sweet and bitter together."

Emma tipped her head, considering how true this was. Through the kitchen window, she spotted Mina crossing the courtyard with an armful of linens. "Does Mina help in the kitchen sometimes too?"

"No, no." Dresia shook her head as she ground almonds with sugar and cinnamon. "Mina is a good cook. But she works too hard already, poor girl. Her family..." She trailed off, speaking rapidly in Arabic to Khadija.

"Like I told you yesterday. My aunt Mina's father is very sick," Khadija explained. "And her brother hurt his arm."

Emma sprinkled the spiced ground almonds over the shredded chicken mixture. "Yes. That must be difficult for them."

"*Na'am*," Dresia agreed. "But Mina is good girl. Honest girl." She met Emma's eyes. "Not like some who drink too much and make trouble."

"Like Mr. Astor?" Emma asked carefully.

Dresia pressed her lips together and turned to check the oven temperature.

"I heard him fighting with Mrs. Ruby and Ms. Fatima," Khadija offered quietly. "Very loud English, very fast. I could not understand."

"When was this?"

"The night before-" Khadija stopped, her eyes widened, and she quickly focused on the tea she was preparing.

Emma watched as the young girl carefully arranged fresh mint leaves in a small glass, added sugar and tea. "Will you show me how to pour it properly?"

Khadija's smile returned. "Yes! You must pour from high up, like this." She demonstrated, creating a foamy head on the tea. "See? Perfect bubbles."

Emma tried, splashing tea on the counter. "Oh no!"

"Is okay," Dresia laughed, handing Khadija a cloth to wipe up the spilled tea.

But Emma took the cloth. "I can clean," she said with a smile.

"Now, watch how we fold the b'stilla." Dresia's capable hands created perfect triangles with the phyllo, sealing in the spiced mixture.

"The sugar and cinnamon on top make it special," Khadija explained as they decorated the finished pie. "We sprinkle it in a pattern, almost like henna." She motioned to Emma's decorated hands.

As the pie baked, Emma tried mixing up a pot of mint tea.

"More sugar," Khadija said, moving the beautifully painted ceramic sugar container toward Emma.

"*Shukran*." Emma practiced pouring again, this time doing it almost perfectly.

When they pulled the golden-brown pastry from the oven, its aroma was intoxicating. Emma cut into it, took a bite and closed her eyes in appreciation. "This is amazing! The way the sweetness blends with the spiced meat..."

"You have good hands for pastry," Dresia nodded approvingly. "Your layers are perfect, like mille feuille."

"Thank you," Emma beamed. "Though I still can't pronounce half the ingredients properly."

"*La bas*," Khadija giggled. "No problem. You learn."

Emma watched as Dresia efficiently cleaned her workspace. "Dresia, you know everything about cooking! Everything that happens in this kitchen..."

"I know enough," Dresia replied, her tone carefully neutral. "I know Mina would never hurt anyone."

Emma carried the warm plate of b'stilla into the salon, pride swelling in her chest at how perfectly it had turned out. Dr. Grant sat hunched over his phone in one of the carved wooden chairs, his leg bouncing rapidly. Emma caught a glimpse of a photo of a woman before he turned it over and set it on the table.

Victor lounged on the cushioned bench, his feet propped up as he scrolled through his phone. "Ah, something smells wonderful!"

"I just learned to make b'stilla," Emma said, setting the plate on the low table. "Would anyone like to try it?"

"Such artistry with the sugar design on top," Victor praised, reaching for a piece. "Almost too beautiful to eat."

Dr. Grant waved off the offer, his attention back on his phone.

"Look at these photos from my desert trip," Victor said, turning his phone to show Emma. "The sunset over the dunes was magnificent."

Emma leaned in to see. "Oh wow, the colors are incredible! And is that your camel?"

"Yes, that's Jasmine. Not mine to own, of course. But I rode her there. Quite temperamental, but she grew on me."

Edith bustled into the room in a bright flowery dress that made her red glasses look subdued. "Are we sharing desert photos? Oh, you must see mine from the High Atlas and Sahara expedition!"

Daniel appeared in the doorway just then, and Emma smiled up at him as he crossed to the table and settled in next to her with a quick kiss.

"Check out what I made!" Emma motioned to the pastry.

Daniel took a bite of the b'stilla. His eyes widened. "Em, this is amazing! The flavors and the texture of the pastry..."

"Dresia taught me," Emma beamed. "Though I doubt I'll be able to recreate it back home without more practice."

"This," Edith said, motioning to her phone, "was our camp at sunset- oh bother, where did those photos go? I just had them, and now- what is this? My flight itinerary? Why are these new phones so hard to manage. If I touch it, it decides to do something new, all on its own."

Emma and Daniel shared a smile as Edith, exasperated, dropped her phone back into her purse.

"And speaking of missing things, I can't find my silver Berber bracelet anywhere!"

Emma saw Daniel's eyes twinkle in amusement. "When did you last have it?"

"Yesterday, I think. That maid, Mina, was cleaning my room..." Edith's voice trailed off suggestively.

"I'm sure Mina didn't steal it," Emma said.

Edith harrumphed. "Well, it didn't lose itself."

Victor leaned forward with another photo. "Here's the Bedouin camp where we stayed." The photo showed several large white tents with the most elaborate interiors Emma had ever seen.

As Victor flipped through photos, Emma's eyes grew wide. There were couches and beds, silver tea sets, and beautiful Moroccan rugs. "That looks incredible," Emma sighed as she squeezed Daniel's hand. "I wish we had time to do something like that before heading back to Minnesota."

Daniel looked from the photo to Emma and smiled as their eyes met. "The stars must be amazing out there."

"Yes. Like diamonds scattered across black silk," Victor confirmed. "Though journalism doesn't pay enough to make such trips often."

"Dr. Grant, have you been to the Sahara?" Emma asked.

The doctor jumped slightly, as if pulled from deep thoughts. "What? Oh, yes. Twice actually."

For some reason, Victor smirked at Dr. Grant, as if this was funny. Dr. Grant scowled and stood abruptly. "If you'll excuse me..."

As Mina entered quietly with a tray to clear the empty plates, he hurried out, and Emma wondered what had him so on edge.

"Where is that bracelet?" Edith said, and Emma saw that the older woman had emptied nearly all the contents of her purse onto the table. "It's the silver one with the tribal designs. You saw it, didn't you, Emma? I'm certain I had it yesterday."

"I'm not sure," Emma said.

"First Mrs. Astor's necklace, now my bracelet," Edith said loudly. "It does make one wonder about the cleaning staff..."

Mina stopped and stared at Edith's back. Although she didn't speak much English, it was clear she'd understood Edith. Her face crumpled and she fled the room, leaving the tray behind.

Victor turned his phone to show another photo. "The camels at sunrise..."

Emma still stared after Mina. Edith Pimm looked around, apparently unaware the maid had been in the room. How could Edith suspect Mina?

Daniel looked at Victor's phone where the Russian, apparently undisturbed by the maid's distress, was still flipping through photos.

"And this is the guide who took us. He was wonderful."

Emma turned to Edith. "Mrs. Pimm, perhaps we should be careful about making accusations. Mina's been through enough with the police questioning."

"Accusations? I merely stated facts. My bracelet is missing." Edith rifled through her purse again.

"But suggesting Mina took it-"

"Well, who else had access to my room?"

Emma took a deep breath. "Maybe we could apologize to her?"

"Apologize? For what? When my bracelet is returned, then we can discuss who should apologize to whom." Edith's red glasses slipped down her nose as she dug through her bag.

After another glance at the doorway where Mina had fled, Emma changed tactics. "How are your cats doing? You must be worried about them."

Edith's face softened. "Oh, Scarlet and Midnight. My babies. They're doing well, although I'm sure they wonder why I lied to them. We talked about this trip before I left, and I showed them- with days on their treat calendar- how long I'd be gone." She shook her head. "Have I shown you pictures of them?"

The door to the small business center opened and Derek stepped out into the salon, his shirt wrinkled. He collapsed onto a couch in the corner looking like he hadn't slept in days. Emma wished there was a natural way to go over to him and ask about his relationship with Ruby.

"I should go check on Jimmy Grant," Victor said, rising smoothly. "See if he's up for a stroll through the city. Good day, ladies."

Emma watched him leave. "Dr. Grant's first name is Jimmy? And Victor seems to be taking the delay well, doesn't he? He seems almost cheerful."

"Oh yes," Edith brightened, her cat photos momentarily forgotten. "Such an interesting man. We spent hours yesterday sharing travel photos. He's been everywhere - the Black Sea, the Seychelles, Thailand, Colombia..."

"The Seychelles?"

There was a grunted swear word from Derek and both women turned to look at him. He closed his eyes and ran a hand through his hair, shaking his head as Khadija handed him a glass of orange juice. "Thanks," he muttered before shooting Emma and Edith a dirty look.

"Islands in the Indian Ocean. Though that was all before..." Edith lowered her voice with a quick glance toward Derek, who was downing the orange juice. "Well. Before he lost everything. Poor man."

Emma frowned. "Lost everything? But he's here on vacation..."

"Oh no, dear. He's writing an article for a Russian travel magazine. Though..." Edith glanced around conspiratorially. "When I asked, he was rather vague about the exact topic of his article."

Mustafa appeared at Derek's side. "Mr. Astor, your fax has arrived."

Derek grunted and hauled himself up, setting his empty juice glass on a brass table.

Once he'd left, Edith leaned closer to Emma. "My room's next to his, you know. The night Ruby died..." She glanced toward the door. "I heard them arguing. Terrible row."

Emma's stomach tightened. "Really? What were they fighting about?"

"Derek was shouting. And Ruby, poor girl, was in tears. He accused her of ruining his business plans. And..." Edith's voice dropped to a whisper. "He said she was cheating on him."

"Cheating?" Emma didn't feel too surprised. Ruby had clearly been unhappy. "Did he say who with?"

"If he did, I didn't hear. And she denied it," Edith whispered. "But, well. He isn't exactly the most thoughtful husband, is he." She gave a small sniff and glanced to the door.

Emma's mind raced. Derek had a motive. But then there was Fatima's disappearance... Could they have worked together? But if so, why would Derek still be here while Fatima fled? Again, she wished there was some excuse to talk to him.

"More tca?" Khadija appeared with a fresh pot and a plate of twisty, sticky pastries.
92

"Oh yes, please," Edith said. "These *sh'bakia* are one of the things I'm going to miss about Morocco when I go home. Which reminds me, I didn't show you my babies. I have photos on my phone." She opened her purse and gasped. "Would you look at that? Here's my bracelet!"

Chapter 9

Emma watched as Edith's face flushed pink and she lifted the silver bracelet from her purse.

"Oh dear. I feel absolutely dreadful." Edith's large red glasses slipped down her nose, and she pushed them up again. "I've been losing everything lately, and now accusing that poor girl. And you told me not to accuse her, didn't you?" She patted Emma's hand. "It's the stress! I've never been involved in a murder before!"

"Murder?" Victor said, stepping back into the salon. His pressed oxford shirt looked fresh despite the Moroccan heat, and his wire-rimmed glasses caught the light as he smiled. "That's a strong word, Ms. Pimm." He pulled out a chair at their table and rejoined them. "I think you are taking on too much stress. Benali will find it was an accident and we will all go home soon. I suggest a rest. I find a good night's sleep does wonders for the perspective."

Emma smoothed her new caftan, still marveling at how the flowing fabric kept her cool as she leaned toward Edith. "Maybe you should go find Mina? I'm sure she'd appreciate an apology."

"Yes, yes of course." Edith stood, adjusting her glasses. "Though I doubt she understood everything I said..."

"She understood enough," Emma said gently.

As Edith hurried off, her comfortable walking shoes squeaking slightly on the tile floor, Emma said, "I thought you were going out in the city with Dr. Grant."

Victor shrugged. "He doesn't want to go out."

Emma saw Daniel slip to the arched doorway where Mustafa stood. The hotel owner's white djellaba seemed to glow in the shaft of afternoon sunlight streaming through the window. They spoke in low voices, Daniel's khaki pants and blue oxford shirt contrasting with Mustafa's traditional dress.

"And you?" Victor asked. "You seem to have done some good shopping. Do you think we will be here now many days longer?"

Emma shook her head. "I don't know. I just hope they find who killed Ruby."

Victor gave her a condescending smile. "Like the old woman, you also think it was murder? They will find no one except maybe a Moroccan street thief, I assure you. Why? Because it was an accident after a break in. That necklace- I ask you. Morocco is a poor country. What did she think would happen?"

Emma stared at him, her heart rate quickening at his arrogance and his suggestion that Ruby was somehow to blame for her own murder because she's worn a beautiful necklace, or that Moroccans were likely to kill a woman for wearing jewelry. "Wearing a necklace does not give anyone a reason to commit murder. And being poor does not make people commit crimes. And I assure you, Mr…" she searched her mind for his last name, "Mr. Novikov, that Ruby's murder was not the result of a break in."

Victor raised his eyebrows and gave her a small smile. "Well, of course, Benali is the one conducting the investigation. We will see what he finds. I think it will not be anything, and we will all go home."

"You seem awfully confident about that." Emma rose, gathering her long red hair over one shoulder. "Enjoy your tea." She crossed the room, catching fragments of Daniel and Mustafa's conversation.

"…at night?" Daniel asked.

"…of course."

As Emma stepped out of the salon, Daniel straightened and cleared his throat. "Is it always this hot in Marrakesh in the summer?"

Mustafa looked confused for a moment. "Hot?" Then his phone chimed in his *djellaba* pocket. He pulled it out, glanced at the screen, and his expression shifted. "Oh. Excuse me, I must take this." He hurried away, his white garment billowing behind him.

"What was that about?" Emma asked, studying Daniel's face.

"I was just asking about local restaurants." Daniel slipped an arm around her waist.

"Really? Because it sounded like you changed the subject as soon as I came over."

Victor's chair scraped against the floor as he stood.

Emma shook her head as she watched him walk out to the garden. Her heart rate was still up from her conversation with him. She waited until he'd left before continuing. "Daniel, if you're working on this investigation, I want to help. We're partners in this, remember?"

Daniel pulled her closer and smiled at her. "Em, of course we're partners. Please don't worry about it. I'm just following up on a few things." He kissed her forehead.

Still irked by Victor's condescending smile and terrible suggestions about Ruby and the Moroccan people, not to mention Daniel's evasive reply, Emma pulled away. "Why can't you tell me what those things are?" She felt her cheeks warm. "You've were gone all day, and now this private conversation..."

"I promise I'll fill you in when I can." Daniel touched her arm, but Emma stepped back.

"That's not the same as including me." She crossed her arms. "I'm so sick of people thinking they know more than me!"

98

Daniel's expression turned sad, and her heart softened. But before she could respond, the heavy wooden door of the hotel creaked open, letting in a blast of hot air and Detective Benali's stocky figure. His white hat with its black brim was slightly askew, and dust clung to his blue uniform.

"Ah, Detective Lindberg." Benali's mustache twitched as his gaze shifted to Emma. "And Ms. Harper."

Emma sighed. The flowing fabric of her caftan caught on her arm bracelet - a souvenir from their morning shopping trip that now felt like it had happened days ago.

Mustafa emerged from his office, the circles under his eyes more pronounced than Emma had seen them before.

"Detective Benali, welcome back." Mustafa's voice sounded exhausted.

Victor stepped in from the garden, his wire-rimmed glasses catching the light. "I knew you would return soon. We can all go home, yes?"

Mina followed Victor, carrying an ornate silver tea service, her dark eyes downcast beneath her hijab. But as Benali turned toward her, she froze. The tea glasses clinked against their silver tray.

"Mina," Mustafa started, but she was already backing away, disappearing into the kitchen with the tea.

Victor's pale green eyes followed her retreat. He straightened his crisp shirt and cleared his throat. "Detective Benali, if I may? That girl - we are all aware her family has been having financial troubles, no? And now this behavior. She is as skittish as a mouse. Or should I say, as a guilty party." He spread his hands. "Perhaps looking into her connections would prove... illuminating?"

Emma's stomach twisted at Victor's insinuation. The way he'd delivered it so smoothly, as if he were merely suggesting a restaurant for dinner rather than potentially ruining someone's life.

Benali rubbed his mustache thoughtfully. "We are pursuing all possibilities, Mr. Novikov."

"Of course, of course." Victor smiled, but it didn't reach his eyes. "I only wish to be helpful."

Emma rolled her eyes and turned away.

Chapter 10

As she climbed the curved staircase, her new caftan swishing against the ornate tiles, Emma's fingers ran along the railing. She was deliberately keeping her pace slow to avoid catching up with Benali.

Was she just frazzled from so many weeks of traveling, Emma wondered. Or was there something up with Daniel's behavior? First he denies being in the market when she was sure she'd seen him, and then the clear topic change with Mustafa. When they'd first met, several months and murders ago, he had tried to keep her from helping with an investigation. But it just wasn't like him anymore. What was he up to?

The second floor's dim hallway was cool, the thick stone walls and breeze from the opening to the garden below providing relief from the Moroccan heat. The orange trees came up, and a gentle breeze came through an open window at the end of the hall.

Was it possible that Daniel didn't trust her to help investigate Ruby's death for some reason? He had trusted her for so long that it felt odd- like stepping back into an old pair of too small shoes- to have him stop confiding in her. Benali's condescending smile and comments about women and gossip came to her mind, followed by Victor's words about Emma and "the old woman" thinking it was murder.

But it was murder- Emma was certain.

Edith emerged from her room, her silver curls slightly disheveled. "Oh, Emma! I've just found my plane ticket. It was in my other handbag all along." She clutched a worn leather purse. "Though I suppose it hardly matters now."

"That's wonderful, Edith."

"I do wish they'd let us leave soon. Midnight gets more and more picky about his food the longer I'm away…" Edith's voice trailed off as she headed toward the stairs.

Emma continued down the hall, passing the door to Ruby's room. She paused when she saw Adeline standing by her own door, fumbling with her room key. Her auburn hair escaped from beneath her silk scarf in waves, and her silver bangles clinked softly.

"Everything alright?" Emma asked.

Adeline's green eyes were rimmed with red. "I keep thinking about Ruby. About our last conversation." She shook her head, her eyes red. "I should have insisted she leave him months ago."

Before Emma could respond, Brian's door opened, and Adeline closed her mouth and turned away. With an apologetic smile at Emma, she slipped into her own room.

Brian emerged, his salt-and-pepper hair uncombed, and without a glance at Emma, crossed
102

the hall to Derek's door. His knuckles rapped against the dark wood.

Emma stepped back into an alcove, partially hidden by a potted palm.

Derek's door creaked open. "What?" His voice was rough.

"We need to talk..." Brian's voice dropped to a harsh whisper.

Emma was turning to go to her own room, embarrassed to be eavesdropping, when she heard the word, "divorce." She turned back to the two men.

"… not your business." Derek's words were almost too quiet to hear.

"It became my business when my daughter ended up dead!" Brian's whisper grew more intense. "If you'd just agreed to-"

"I said I don't want to talk about it!" Derek pushed past Brian, and his door slammed.

As he stormed toward the stairs, another door opened, and Detective Benali emerged – not from Ruby's room as Emma had expected, but from Fatima's.

Benali adjusted his white hat with its black brim. "Ah, Ms. Harper." He nodded to her. The looking up the hallway, "Mr. Johnson," he said to Brian, "Just who I was hoping to find. May I have a moment of your time?"

Brian slumped down the hall, reminding Emma of a dried leaf being pushed along the sidewalk. "Please tell me you have some news."

"Of a fashion, yes. We identified Ruby's fingerprints on a glass of mint tea from Fatima's room from yesterday." Benali's mustache twitched. "And now, this." He held up a crumpled piece of paper.

Brian sank into one of the carved wooden chairs that lined the hallway, his polo shirt damp with sweat. "What is it?"

"From the trash can in Fatima's bathroom. A note to written someone about going to Casablanca. Never delivered, clearly." Benali's eyes narrowed. "Her cell phone was left behind as well."

Emma's gaze darted between the two men.

"I fear Fatima might have fled the country," Benali continued. "Abandoning her phone so she can't be traced."

Brian's face had gone chalk white. "No, no – she would never do that. Not Fatima. She's from Casablanca. She was probably just going home."

Benali's posture stiffened. "She's from Casablanca? Why didn't you tell me this before? When I asked for her information, you said you didn't have her address, only her cell number."

Emma's eyebrows went up. Brian and Fatima were business partners. Of course Brian would have her contact information. The hallway fell silent. Brian's fingers gripped the arms of his chair, his knuckles white.

"Mr. Johnson?" Benali prompted.

Brian pulled a business card from his wallet with trembling fingers. "Here. Her address and home phone number in Casablanca."

"You had this all along," Emma whispered in a matter-of-fact tone, and Benali looked at her in surprise.

But Brian's gaze was fixed on the stone floor tiles.

"What else have you forgotten to tell me, Mr. Johnson?" Benali asked.

Brian shook his head, but Benali took him by the arm and escorted him to his room.

"We will have a talk now, you and I," Benali said as Brian, hands trembling, unlocked his door and the two men stepped inside.

The door clicked shut behind them and Emma, avoiding the temptation to press her ear to the door, went to lie down.

Chapter 11

In the hotel kitchen, the aroma of honey and spices seemed to be everywhere. Dresia stood at a large wooden table, her traditional dress pristine despite the flour dusting the surface. Khadija perched on a stool nearby and smiled shyly at Emma, her silver hoop earrings catching the morning light that streamed through the high windows.

"Good morning," Emma said, pulling her red hair into a neat bun. "Or I should say, *sabah el kheir*. Is that right?"

When Dresia looked up surprised, and Khadija broke into a wide grin, Emma couldn't help smiling. "I got it right?"

"*Sabah el kheir!*" Dresia replied with a smile as she greeted Emma.

"I'm not too early?"

Khadija shook her head. "No, no. Dresia says we start now." She adjusted her headscarf and hopped down from the stool.

Dresia smiled and gestured to the ingredients laid out on the table. "First, we toast the sesame seeds and almonds."

Emma watched as Dresia demonstrated, the seeds turning golden in the pan. The kitchen was alive with the sounds of pots clanking and the whoosh of gas burners.

"Now we grind them together," Khadija said, as Dresia poured the toasted mixture into a food processor.

"It's like making a very fancy cookie dough," Emma observed, thinking of her bakery back home.

Khadija giggled. "Not just a cookie. *Sh'bakia* is special."

They worked the dough together, Emma's hands covered in flour as she helped knead the spice-scented mixture. The morning sun cast patterns through the intricate metalwork of the kitchen windows onto the tiled floor.

"Now comes the hard part," Khadija said, watching Dresia demonstrate the complex folding technique. "You must make the flower shape. *Sh'bakia* is not straight."

Emma's first attempt at folding the dough into the traditional flower pattern looked more like the crumpled note Benali had found in Fatima's trash can. Dresia laughed kindly and showed her again, her practiced hands moving with grace.

"Like this," Khadija demonstrated with her own piece of dough. "See? Through here, then pull."

"Oh!" Emma's second attempt looked slightly better. "It's nothing like making cinnamon rolls."

"What is cinnamon rolls?" Khadija asked, her brown eyes curious.

As Emma described her bakery's signature pastry, Dresia nodded approvingly at Emma's improving technique with the sh'bakia.

"Mina loves *sh'bakia*," Khadija said softly, arranging finished pastries on a tray. "She is too sick today."

"I hope she feels better soon," Emma replied, focusing on folding another piece of dough.

When the folded pieces were fried, the kitchen filled with the sweet scent of the honey and orange blossom water Dresia began heating over the stove. Emma watched in fascination as the fried pastries were dipped in the fragrant syrup, emerging golden and glistening. Khadija and Emma sprinkled them with more toasted sesame seeds.

"These are beautiful," Emma said, admiring the finished *sh'bakia*. "I never imagined I'd learn to make something like this."

Khadija beamed with pride as she translated Emma's words to Dresia, who responded with a stream of Arabic.

"She says you have good hands for pastry," Khadija translated. "Even if they are American hands."

Emma laughed, rinsing honey from her fingers. "*Shukran*, Dresia. This is so different from anything I make at home."

Emma balanced the plate of *sh'bakia* as she walked through the carved archways, her fingers still slightly sticky with traces of honey. Her pastries had turned out beautifully twisted and golden, though not quite as perfect as Dresia's. She spotted Daniel emerging from the business center, his blue oxford shirt sleeves rolled up to his elbows.

"Hey! Want to try what I made?" She held up the plate, proud of her morning's work.

Daniel's eyes lit up. "I always want to taste anything you make. What are they called again?"

"*Sh'bakia*. Dresia and Khadija taught me how to make them. They're incredibly different from anything I've made before." Emma watched his face as he tasted one and smiled when he closed his eyes in delight. "What have you been up to?"

"Just hanging out. Talking to people." He licked his fingers and selected another pastry from the plate.

Emma glanced through the business center's open door. The room was empty, computer screens dark. "I don't see anyone else in there."

"I needed to send an email." He took a bite of the second *sh'bakia*. "These are heavenly!"

Emma paused. "You have your laptop upstairs." Emma shifted the plate to her other hand, leaving a faint honey print on the ceramic. "Daniel, can you please just tell me what you're doing? Is this about the case?"

He looked surprised. "No. Emma-"

"You're having conversations with people-people involved in the case, like that gem dealer in

the market. I thought we were past this after that
first murder back in Whispering Pines."

Before Daniel could respond, rapid footsteps
approached. Khadija darted past them, chasing after
an orange striped cat. "*La, la! Ajee!*"

"Oh!" Emma was so surprised she almost
dropped the plate of *sh'bakia*. "I understood what
Khadija said! *La* means 'no,' and *ajee* means 'come
here! That was almost like a complete sentence!"

Daniel stepped back as the cat streaked by
again.

"That's Edith's stray." Emma set down the
plate and moved to help. "Mustafa told her not to
feed the cats. They aren't allowed in the hotel. But
she's been feeding it. Here kitty..."

The cat darted under an intricately carved
table. While Emma and Khadija tried to coax it out,
Daniel's phone buzzed. He glanced at the screen and
stepped away.

"I need to take this," he said, already
heading toward the garden. "We'll talk later. Love
you!"

Emma looked up, watching him disappear
through the carved wooden doors into the sunlit
courtyard. Her stomach twisted with frustration as
she wondered what he wasn't telling her.

"Ah!" Khadija triumphantly scooped up the
cat. "We caught him. Thank you for helping."

But Emma barely heard her, still staring at
the garden entrance Daniel had vanished through.

Emma waited until Daniel was well out of sight before slipping into the business center herself. She could do a little sleuthing of her own and see if she could tell what he's been doing.

The small room smelled of toner and electronics, its walls decorated in a line of tile mosaics. A single computer monitor sat in the dim light filtering through the latticed window screens.

She ran her fingers along the keyboard and when she clicked the space bar, the monitor lit up. She checked the browser history, but it was empty. She ran a hand over the still-warm printer and leaned toward the wall to get a better look at it, her long red hair falling forward.

"What were you doing in here?" she muttered.

Something caught her eye - a corner of paper peeking out from behind the desk. Emma reached for it, bangles jingling as she reached behind the desk, her fingers stretching to close around what turned out to be a spiral notebook, its cover worn, and pages dog-eared. Not Daniel's tidy style at all.

She flipped it open. Her eyes widened as she scanned the pages filled with angular handwriting:

Tuesday evening, Ruby with Derek. Separate rooms (314, 316).

Wednesday morning, walk through medina. Lunch with Adeline at Cafe Atlas. Evening visit to

Jemaa el-Fnaa, shopping in souks. Ruby bought gold bracelet.

The notes continued, detailing Ruby's movements with times and locations. Emma's heartbeats quickened as she turned page after page of meticulous observations.

"Oh, my gosh," she whispered. The precise, angular script was distinctive and unfamiliar.

After a quick glance over her shoulder, she laid the notebook open and the desk, pulled out her phone, and photographed each page. Her hands shook slightly as she turned the pages and realized what this meant. Someone had been stalking Ruby. She thought about who else she'd seen using this room.

Derek had been in here earlier, possibly sending a fax. But why would he track his wife's movements so carefully? He would have been with her. And there was the first entry- *Ruby with Derek. Separate rooms (314, 316).* That wouldn't make sense if Derek was the one writing.

Emma slipped the notebook into her shoulder bag, adjusting the strap. She needed to get this to Benali.

She started toward the garden to tell Daniel but stopped. He was doing his own investigating. Did that mean he didn't want to work with her? Maybe she should take the notebook to the police station by herself.

Through the arched doorway, she could see Daniel still talking on his cell phone. She was being silly. For all she knew, he was changing their flights. Friday was clearly not going to work. But whatever he was doing, he wasn't available right now. And Benali needed to see the notebook.

With a sigh, she headed for the hotel entrance alone. As she passed the salon's ornate doorway, voices drifted out - one male, one female.

"...can't believe you'd even..." That was Derek's voice, tight with anger.

"But surely you must see..." Adeline's cultured British accent replied, but the rest was lost in the bubbling of the fountain.

Emma leaned against the cool tile wall beside the door, straining to hear more, but their voices had dropped too low. She clutched her bag containing the notebook closer to her side and continued toward the hotel entrance.

A crash in the salon made Emma whirl around.

Chapter 12

Emma rushed through the arched doorway to the salon, her sandals skidding on the polished stone floor.

Adeline stood, her turquoise caftan rippling around her, while her carved wooden chair lay toppled behind her. Derek loomed over her, his linen shirt wrinkled and his dark hair disheveled.

"You killed her!" Adeline's voice cracked. "You couldn't stand that she was going to leave you!"

"That's insane." Derek's jaw clenched and he raised his hand. "I loved Ruby."

Daniel rushed in from the garden, shoving his phone into his pocket. "What's going on?"

Emma stepped between Derek and Adeline, placing a hand on Derek's chest and another on Adeline's arm. "Derek, stop! Let's all sit down and talk about this calmly."

"He came in here," Adeline's green eyes flashed, "and started talking about dinner plans! As if nothing even happened! As if Ruby wasn't…" Adeline hiccupped. "I don't even think he cares! I think he's happy she's out of his hair!"

Emma guided Adeline to a plush cushioned sofa while Daniel righted the fallen chair and Derek lowered his hand and sat, staring at Adeline with anger.

Emma had been wishing for a way to talk to Derek about Ruby, and now the opportunity was right in front of her. The notebook could wait.

"Shut up!" Derek said. "you don't know anything!"

"Of course I do," Adeline said. "I was her best friend."

Daniel sat in the seat next to Derek. "Derek, why don't you tell us what we don't know?" Daniel said. "It might help to talk about it."

Derek sank back into his chair, staring at Adeline. "What's to tell?"

"What about your marriage? You had separate rooms here."

Derek's shoulders slumped and he looked down. "That was Ruby's choice."

"And why was that?" Adeline shot back.

Derek said loudly, "I would say to ask her, but-"

"Oh honestly!" Adeline shouted, and Emma put a hand on her arm.

"The threatening note she received," Emma pressed. "Do you know who sent it? Did she mention it to you?"

"No." His response was clipped, and he shut his mouth in a tight line.

Emma sat back. This was not exactly the conversation she'd hoped for. "Ok. She didn't tell you about the note. And what about Fatima?" She watched his face carefully. "Do you know why she left? Were you two close?"

His expression went blank. "We had no relationship, close or otherwise. She worked for Brian."

"Is that all?" Emma asked, watching him for any sign of deception.

For the first time, he looked up from the floor and met her gaze. He squinted at her through red eyes. "I don't know what you're talking about. But I loved my wife, and I didn't kill her."

Emma softened her gaze. "The ruby necklace that's missing," she said gently. "That was a gift from you?"

He looked back at the floor. "It was a wedding present. Seven years ago." Suddenly, he stood. "I don't have to answer any more questions. This is ridiculous. It's bad enough dealing with Benali." He strode out, hands shaking.

Emma turned to Adeline, who had collapsed into silent tears.

"He's lying," Adeline whispered.

Derek's footsteps faded up the stone staircase.

Adeline's silk scarf had slipped from her hair. "Derek knows exactly why Ruby wanted separate rooms. He was horrible to her, constantly criticizing everything she did. You saw how he laughed at her fortune."

Emma settled deeper into the embroidered cushions. "What do you mean?"

"He mocked her interests, her clothes, even the way she arranged flowers." Adeline's silver bangles clinked as she gestured. "Nothing was ever good enough for him. I'm surprised he didn't criticize the way she died."

Daniel leaned forward in his chair. "And what about Fatima? There wasn't anything between her and Derek?"

"Oh no," Adeline shook her head. "Fatima and Brian are the ones who are together."

Emma's eyes widened. "Fatima and Brian?" She remembered seeing them getting into that taxi together near the spice shops.

"Yes, and it made Ruby furious." Adeline's voice dropped. "Ruby's mother died when Ruby was young. She wanted her father to remain loyal to her mother's memory."

Emma thought of the argument she'd overheard between Ruby and Fatima. "I heard them arguing."

"Ruby didn't know until this trip. She was really angry with Fatima for lying to her. And worried about her inheritance. She thought Fatima might convince Brian to change his will." Adeline pulled her scarf back over her hair. "Ruby needed that money if she was going to leave Derek."

Emma studied Adeline's face, noting the genuine grief in her eyes. "How long have you and Ruby been friends?"

A small smile touched Adeline's lips. "Since eighth grade. We met at boarding school in Switzerland. We were both so homesick at first. We arrived the same year." She twisted one of her bangles. "After graduation, we used to meet up during university breaks, take trips together."

Emma smiled. "That sounds wonderful. What kind of trips?"

"Oh, lovely adventures." Adeline wiped her eyes. "We hiked to Everest Base Camp in Nepal." Adeline smiled. "And that amazing week in Santiago, Chile. Oh my gosh, the fruit. But I always regretted not going with her to the Seychelles. That was ten years ago this month."

Emma sat up straighter. "The Seychelles? That's the second time I've heard about that place. I'd never even heard of it before."

"It's a gorgeous little chain of islands in the Indian Ocean." Adeline's voice grew wistful. "Ruby went right after college."

Emma shook her head, marveling. "This trip is opening my eyes to how much of the world I haven't seen. Back in Whispering Pines, the most exotic destination anyone talks about is Disney World."

"There's so much out there to explore," Adeline agreed. She reached for her cup of mint tea, her hand trembling slightly. "and Ruby was always up for an adventure. She and I were supposed to go to Istanbul next month."

Emma replayed Adeline's words. The Seychelles. And Ruby's fortune. She'd almost forgotten about that. Emma hadn't seen Amira recently. Could the fortune teller have slipped away?

Chapter 13

Emma adjusted her new blue caftan, grateful for the light fabric in the afternoon heat. She'd pulled her red hair up into a loose bun to keep it off her neck. The notebook felt heavy in her embroidered leather bag as she and Daniel made their way through the winding streets of the medina. She'd told him about it after their conversation with Adeline.

"These alleys are like a maze," Emma said, following Daniel and ducking under a string of brass lanterns hanging across their path. "Don't you need your phone? How do you know which way to go?"

Daniel's blue oxford shirt already showing dark patches of sweat. "I memorized the route when I walked it earlier. The police station is near the main square."

Emma clutched the tin of *sh'bakia*. So, he'd been to the police station without her. She would figure out what he was up to yet. "I hope these survive the heat," she said. As Emma spoke, she was noticing landmarks along the route. If Daniel could learn his way around this ancient city, she could too.

They emerged from a narrow alley into bright sunlight. The Jemaa el-Fnaa spread before them, alive with activity. Snake charmers' flutes wailed over the general bustle while smoke rose from food stalls.

"Just down that side street." Daniel pointed to a sand-colored building with Morocco's red and green flag hanging limp in the still air.

Inside, the temperature dropped dramatically. A ceiling fan whirred overhead as they approached the front desk where one of Benali's assistants named Mohammed sat.

"Good afternoon," Emma smiled. "We're here to see Detective Benali."

The young Mohammed looked up from his paperwork. Before he could respond, Benali's voice carried from down the hall.

"Ah, Ms. Harper, Mr. Lindberg." Benali called, mustache twitching as he noticed the tin in Emma's hands. "What brings you here today?"

"We brought you something," Emma held up the tin. "*Sh'bakia*. And we found something you should see."

Benali's eyes lit up at the sight of the treats. "How wonderful. That is too kind of you. Please, come into my office."

He led them down a hallway into a small room with windows overlooking the square. A desk dominated the space, covered in stacks of papers and files. Benali gestured to two chairs facing his desk.

Emma opened the tin. "I made the *sh'bakia* this morning with Dresia."

Emma watched as Benali selected one of the twisted, honey-soaked pastries from the tin. His eyes widened as he bit into it.

"These are excellent. One of my favorite sweets. We usually eat them during Ramadan, but I welcome *sh'bakia* any time. You learned from Dresia? She is an excellent cook." He reached for another.

"Yes, this morning." Emma pulled the notebook from her bag. "But we also found something you need to see. I discovered this behind the desk in the hotel's business center."

Benali set down his half-eaten *sh'bakia*, rose to rinse his hands in a sink against the wall, and took the notebook. He flipped through the pages, his expression growing more serious with each turn.

"This is quite detailed. Times, places, even conversations." He looked up at Emma. "Where exactly did you find this?"

"It had fallen behind the desk."

"Interesting." Benali studied one page intently. "These notes go back to when they first arrived in Marrakesh."

Emma leaned forward. "Someone was apparently stalking Ruby."

Benali's mustache twitched. "Perhaps."

"I agree with Emma," Daniel said.

Emma gave him a grateful look and shifted in his chair. "The handwriting could help identify who wrote it."

123

"Indeed. It is distinct." Benali opened a desk drawer, pulled out a clear evidence bag, and carefully placed the notebook inside. "Thank you for bringing this to my attention." He placed it on top of a case file.

Emma noticed that he directed his words to Daniel rather than her. She straightened in her chair. "There's something else you should know. Adeline told me that Ruby and Derek were having serious problems. Ruby was considering leaving him."

"Yes, I am aware. And did she say why?"

"According to Adeline, Derek treated Ruby poorly. And Ruby was worried about her inheritance being threatened by her father's relationship with Fatima."

Benali's pen scratched across his notepad. "This matches with what we learned about the argument overheard the night of the murder."

Mohammed appeared in the doorway, his navy uniform crisp despite the heat. He beckoned to Benali.

"One moment, please." Benali dabbed honey from his mustache with a handkerchief and followed his assistant into the hall.

As soon as the door clicked shut, Emma's gaze fell on the case file beneath the notebook they'd brought in. She glanced at Daniel, who was already reaching for it.

"Quick," she whispered, leaning forward in her chair to see better as Daniel flipped it open.

124

The file contained photographs of Ruby's room and several printed pages in unfamiliar Arabic script. Beneath those were several pages of text messages in English, apparently taken from Fatima's abandoned phone. Emma's heart raced as she scanned the exchanges between Fatima and Brian:

"Ruby cannot find out about us," one message from Fatima read. "It would destroy her."

Brian's response: "I know. But I can't keep lying to my daughter."

Emma's eyes widened at Fatima's next text: "Don't worry. I have a solution. Let me handle this."

Daniel's fingers tensed on the paper. Before they could read more, footsteps approached in the hallway. Daniel quickly closed the file and set it back exactly as it had been, just as the door handle turned.

Emma smoothed her caftan and tried to look casual as Benali entered, his white hat tucked under his arm.

"Have you had any luck finding Fatima?" Emma asked.

Benali settled back behind his desk, replacing his hat on the corner. "I cannot discuss details of an ongoing investigation." He pressed a button on his desk phone. "But perhaps you would join me for mint tea with these excellent *sh'bakia*?"

"That would be lovely," Emma said, though her mind was racing with questions about those text messages.

"Yes, thank you," Daniel added, his eyes darting to the case file.

Benali spoke rapid Arabic into the phone. Emma caught the word "*atay*" which she remembered meant tea. She was proud of recognizing even that one word, though she wished she understood what else was being said and what was written in the file.

As Daniel and Benali discussed travels in Morocco, Emma glanced down and admired the embroidered hem of her new blue caftan and sipped her mint tea. The police station's worn wooden chairs weren't particularly comfortable, but the tea was perfect - sweet and fragrant.

"Have you visited Fez?" Benali asked, breaking a piece of *sh'bakia*. "The medina there is even older than ours in Marrakesh."

"Not yet," Daniel said. "Though we met someone staying at our hotel who lives there."

"Ah yes, the British woman." Benali nodded. "Adeline."

The detective, Emma thought, missed nothing. "What about the Atlas Mountains?" she asked. "Are they as beautiful as everyone says?"

"More beautiful." Benali's mustache twitched with a smile. "The cedar forests, the valleys filled with flowers, the Berber villages-"

126

A knock at the door interrupted him. To Emma's surprise, the woman from the herb shop in the medina entered, her colorful caftan swishing as she walked.

"Ah, Zahra." Benali stood. "*Shukran*."

Today Zahra's dark hair was covered with an indigo head scarf embroidered with silver thread. Emma gave her a small wave, uncertain if the shop owner would recognize her.

But Zahra's face broke into a smile. "Hello again!" she looked between Daniel and Emma, her eyes twinkling. "Did you try my love potion? I think it's working!"

Emma laughed, but the woman's expression turned serious as she looked at Benali.

"About the blue thistle," Zahra said, her voice low and melodious. "It is used in traditional medicine, yes, but it is very dangerous. One of the most poisonous plants in Morocco."

Benali's expression tightened. He glanced at Emma and Daniel before turning back to Zahra. "Um, right. Thank you for sharing that. In English." He sighed before shaking his head and smiling. "Would you care to join us for tea and *sh'bakia*?"

"Another time, perhaps. My daughter is waiting outside. But thank you." Zahra's bracelets jangled as she adjusted her scarf and raised a hand. "*Ma'a salama*. Come back to see me in my shop any time."

After she left, Emma set down her teacup. "Blue thistle?"

Benali sighed heavily, running a hand over his face. "I had hoped to keep this quiet for now. But since you overheard - the autopsy results came back this morning. Mrs. Astor was poisoned before receiving the head injury."

"Poisoned?" Emma stared.

"Yes. The blow to her head was meant to disguise the true cause of death. I had hoped..." Benali shook his head. "I had hoped this was a simple robbery gone wrong. But now there is no question. It was murder."

"And the poison was this blue thistle plant?" Daniel asked.

"According to the toxicology report. I needed to confirm with Zahra if it was potent enough to be lethal." Benali picked up his teacup but didn't drink. "Unfortunately, she has just confirmed what I feared."

Emma's mind went to Ruby's fingerprints on the glass in Fatima's room, and then to the lipstick on the glass in Ruby's room. The mauve color, she realized, was exactly the shade Fatima wore.

Chapter 14

Emma stepped out of the police station into the late afternoon heat, squinting against the bright sunlight. The sounds and scents of the Jemaa el-Fnaa washed over her - drums beating, voices calling, smoke from food stalls drifting on the breeze. She adjusted the flowing sleeve of her caftan, grateful for the light fabric and loose fit.

Daniel touched her elbow. "This way is quickest back to the hotel."

Emma smiled. "I remember."

They wound through narrow streets past the shops displaying brass lamps and colorful carpets. A cat darted between Emma's feet.

"Careful." Daniel steadied her with a hand on her shoulder.

As they rounded a corner, Daniel suddenly stopped. A man in a crisp white djellaba stood in the shadows of an archway, beckoning to him.

"Em, wait here a minute?" Daniel's blue eyes met hers briefly before he strode over to the man.

Emma watched as they spoke in hushed tones, the stranger's hands moving animatedly as he talked. Daniel nodded several times. The conversation lasted only a few minutes before Daniel rejoined her.

"Who is that?" Emma brushed a strand of red hair from her face. "Is he involved in the investigation?"

"Oh, just someone I met earlier. He was reminding me the way back to the hotel." Daniel gestured ahead. "The spice market smells amazing, doesn't it?"

Emma frowned at the obvious deflection. "Daniel, you were not getting directions. You are a terrible liar. What are you really doing?"

"Nothing to worry about." He smiled as he took her hand, his palm warm against hers. "Should we stop for some fresh orange juice before heading back?"

Emma pulled her hand away. "I don't want orange juice. I want to know why you won't tell me what you're working on."

"Em, please. Trust me." Daniel's eyes were on hers. "I promise everything will make sense."

Emma sighed as she followed Daniel through the narrow streets of the medina. Her practical walking sandals clicked against the cobblestones as she gathered her thoughts. She tucked a strand of red hair behind her ear. "I think I know who killed Ruby."

Daniel's stride faltered. "What do you mean?"

"Fatima and Brian were having an affair. And earlier in the day, the day Ruby died, I saw them leaving the area near Zahra's shop - where they sell all those traditional medicines and herbs." Emma lowered her voice as they passed a group of tourists. "Including blue thistle, apparently."

Daniel's expression was troubled, but he said, "That's circumstantial at best."

"Then why did Fatima disappear in the middle of the night? Brian claims she just went home to Casablanca, but then why didn't he tell Benali where she lives? And what if Benali's right and she fled the country? And you saw the texts between her and Brian. A solution?"

They paused to let a man pushing cart loaded with vegetables pass.

"If Brian was involved, why would he stay behind?" Daniel shook his head. "And why would he ask us to investigate?"

"Maybe he didn't know what Fatima planned." Emma stepped around a group of children kicking a ball. "What if Brian didn't realize what her solution would be?"

"But the necklace-"

"I think it was taken to make it look like a break-in, just like the broken glass and the head injury." Emma grabbed Daniel's arm as a moped sped past, almost hitting him. "Or maybe Brian wasn't involved. Maybe Fatima acted alone."

"That's not a bad theory." He paused walking as his blue eyes studied her face. "But we need more than theories."

"I'll bet anything the evidence is there. The fingerprints. The lipstick that Benali didn't want to hear about. Even the broken tea service." Emma counted off the points on her fingers. "And Brian's been acting strange - especially since Benali mentioned finding Fatima's phone. I really think he knows something."

They emerged into a small square where the scent of grilled meat and spices filled the air. Daniel guided them toward a quieter side street.

"Do you want to get some lunch?

Emma glanced at the grilled kabobs and nodded, her stomach growling.

Daniel pulled out a chair for her before sitting beside her and saying quietly, "His own daughter? Em, I understand why you're connecting these dots, but-"

"But what? You don't think I could be right?" Emma felt her earlier frustration returning. "Or you just don't want to discuss it because you're working on something else you won't tell me about?"

Daniel ran a hand through his light brown hair. "Please, Em. That's not fair."

"Neither is shutting me out."

She saw him swallow hard as a young boy handed them both menus in English. She could tell from the look on his face that he was worried about something. But what?

Emma's sandals dragged against the worn stone steps as she and Daniel reached the Hotel al Zuhur. The afternoon heat had wilted her hair, and even her caftan was clinging to her. She longed for the cool interior of the riad.

"I still think-" she started, but Daniel was already reaching for the carved wooden door. He squeezed her hand.

"One minute, Em. I need to use the restroom."

She watched him disappear into the hotel's dimness, her hands on her hips. A crumpled paper cup from their stop at a juice stand earlier still dangled from her fingers and she veered toward the hotel's side alley where the dumpster sat.

The narrow space between buildings was in shadow, high walls blocking most of the intense Moroccan sun. Emma wrinkled her nose at the smell as she approached the metal dumpster. As she tossed the cup, something caught her eye - a flash of red, glinting in a stray beam of sunlight that penetrated between the buildings.

Emma froze. It was blood red. Ruby red.

She bent forward, her nose objecting to the smells, and reached. There, partially buried under food scraps, orange peels, and discarded paper, her fingers grasped something cool and hard. She lifted the delicate strand. It was Ruby's necklace.

The gemstones sparkled in the one beam of light like drops of blood.

"Oh my gosh," she whispered.

The necklace - the one supposedly stolen during the break-in - had been thrown away like trash. Emma's mind raced. If someone had killed Ruby for the necklace, they wouldn't have discarded it. Not only was Ruby poisoned before she was hit over the head, but this proved that the necklace had not been the motive.

Fatima, Emma thought, even more certain than before. The pieces fit. The woman had been desperate enough to stay with Brian that she had staged a break in, killed the only woman who her lover cared about enough to threaten her relationship, then disposed of the evidence, and fled the country. And she had seemed so nice at dinner. Emma shuddered.

Careful not to touch the necklace any more than necessary, Emma pulled a tissue from her purse. The delicate gold chain was heavy in her palm as she cradled it in the tissue. Up close, she could see the intricate metalwork that held each ruby in place. It had to have cost a small fortune.

"Oh, Ruby," she murmured, seeing the young woman's worried face again in her mind.

Emma hurried back toward the hotel entrance, the tissue-wrapped necklace clutched tightly in her hand.

She slipped in through the hotel's heavy wooden door, letting her eyes adjust to the relative darkness. The cool fountain bubbled in the garden. Now she just had to find Daniel and show him what she'd discovered. Then they could take it straight to Benali.

But a commotion from the salon caught her attention. As she stepped forward, through the carved archway, she saw several figures clustered on the floor.

"Get some water!" Daniel's voice carried across the marble tiles.

Emma stepped forward. The sight stopped her cold.

Fatima lay sprawled across the carpet, her purple suit jacket beneath her. Daniel knelt beside her, two fingers pressed to her neck. Mina hovered nearby, wringing her hands in her pale blue uniform. And Mustafa was speaking rapidly into his phone in Arabic.

"What happened?" Emma's voice came out as a whisper.

Daniel glanced up. His blue eyes met hers. "Mina says she just collapsed."

Khadija darted forward with a glass of water, her dark hair swishing with the movement. "Here, here," she said.

Daniel shook his head. "She can't."

"Is she- she's not... dead?"

Emma's fingers clenched around the tissue-wrapped necklace in her hand. Fatima - the woman she'd just been accusing of murder - was here. Not fled to Casablanca, not out of the country, but right here in the hotel. And now...

"Not dead," Daniel said. "But I can hardly feel her pulse."

Mustafa said, "The doctor is coming. And I have called Officer Benali as well."

Emma stood frozen in the archway, the weight of Ruby's necklace heavy in her hand. Her mind reeled as everything she thought she knew about Ruby's murder suddenly shifted.

Chapter 15

Emma's fingers clenched around the tissue-wrapped necklace in her hand. Fatima - the woman she'd just been accusing of murder - was here. Not fled to Casablanca or out of the country, but right here in the hotel.

"Doctor!" Emma said. "We have a doctor here. I'll get Dr. Grant." She raced up the stairs and pounded on Dr. Grant's door. "Dr. Grant! Emergency downstairs!"

The door flew open. Dr. Grant's silver hair stuck up at odd angles, and his shirt was half-untucked. "What happened?"

"Fatima's collapsed in the salon. Daniel says he can barely find a pulse."

His face paled. "Dear God, not another one." He pushed her aside and rushed down the stairs.

Dr. Grant dropped to his knees beside Fatima's still form.

"Her pulse is thready," Dr. Grant announced. He pulled out his phone. "I'm calling an ambulance." His hands shook as he dialed.

"Where was everyone when this happened?" Dr. Grant asked when he'd handed the phone to Mustafa to give directions to emergency services. "Who found her?"

"I was coming in from outside," Emma said. "Daniel and Mustafa were already here with her when I walked in."

"And the others?" Dr. Grant's voice cracked.

Mustafa paced beside Fatima and Dr. Grant. "Edith was in the garden reading. Derek's been in his room all afternoon. Brian was- I think also in his room, I'm not sure."

"And Victor?" Dr. Grant asked.

Mustafa shook his head. "I haven't seen Victor."

"Victor's upstairs in his room," Edith said from the doorway. "I saw him go up about an hour ago."

Emma's mind flashed back to an earlier conversation when Edith had talked about Victor. He had visited the Seychelles. And Ruby had visited the Seychelles. Emma's thoughts skidded to a halt.

Could there be a connection? Had something happened between Ruby and Victor in the Seychelles all those years ago? Something worth killing over?

Emma shook her head. It was highly unlikely. Besides, Victor had been in the Sahara the night Ruby died. She'd seen his photos from the trip. Clearly the stress of everything was getting to her.

The wail of approaching sirens cut through her thoughts.

138

Emma watched as paramedics wheeled Fatima down the narrow alley on a stretcher toward the wider street where the ambulance could get through. Dr. Grant walked alongside as they carried Fatima out, rattling off medical terms Emma didn't understand. The ambulance's flashing lights cast red reflected off the ancient walls.

Footsteps on the tile floor made her turn. Victor descended the stairs, his wire-rimmed glasses catching the afternoon light.

"What's happening?" Victor asked. "I heard sirens."

"Fatima collapsed." Emma said, watching his reaction. "They're taking her to the hospital."

"How awful." Victor looked shocked and shook his head. "First Ruby, now this." He walked to the front door and looked out at the lights bouncing off the walls.

Emma settled onto one of the cushioned benches in the salon. "I keep thinking about happier places to take my mind off everything," she said, hoping she wasn't about to be too obvious. "Like those beautiful islands you mentioned visiting - the Seychelles? I'd never even heard of them before."

Victor turned, his eyebrows lifted. "The Seychelles? Ah yes, paradise on Earth." A smile spread across his face. "Crystal waters, pristine beaches, giant tortoises lumbering along..."

"It sounds lovely."

Victor raised an eyebrow. "Is this really the time for your mind to be on vacations? Another woman has died."

"She's not dead," Emma said. "She's still alive."

"Oh!" Victor nodded. "Well, that's a relief to hear." He let out a breath and nodded. "Yes, quite a relief."

"So, when were you there?" Emma kept her tone casual. "The Seychelles, I mean. I'd love to visit someday."

"Oh, it's been..." Victor's eyes were focused back out the open door. He was quiet, staring. Then he shook himself and looked back at Emma. "About ten years now, actually. July, if I remember correctly. Before everything changed." His smile faded. "But even if Miss Fatima is alive, clearly she is not well. Perhaps this isn't the time for vacation stories."

"No, please." Emma leaned forward. "I could use the distraction. What was it like there ten years ago?"

"The most perfect place." Victor said. "I stayed on Mahé island at a small resort. The beaches were practically empty back then - not like now with all the tourists. I spent my mornings snorkeling among the coral reefs."

"Sounds magical." Emma's heart pounded. Ten years ago. July. Exactly when Ruby had been there. "Were there many other guests at your resort?"

"A few." Victor adjusted his glasses. "But not many. I kept to myself mostly. Writing, you know. If you'll excuse me, I'm going to talk to Dr. Grant, to check on poor Fatima."

"Of course."

Emma watched him go, noting the slight stiffness in his shoulders. He'd seemed genuinely surprised when she brought up the Seychelles. But his quick desire to end the conversation made her wonder what - or who - he might be avoiding discussing.

Chapter 16

Emma watched from the doorway as Benali, looking tired, settled into one of the low chairs in the salon, his leather-bound notebook balanced on his knees. His two assistants stationed themselves near the entrance.

"Please, everyone stay close," Benali called out. "I need to speak with each of you."

Dr. Grant went first, dropping heavily onto the cushions across from Benali. His face was drawn. "She's stable, but it was close. The hospital will run tests to see what happened."

"And you were where when she collapsed?"

"In my room, reviewing work emails." Dr. Grant rubbed his temples. "Emma came to get me, and I came down."

Emma leaned against the doorframe, watching as Edith settled into the chair Dr. Grant had vacated. Edith's pastel flowered dress clashed with the deep reds and golds of the Moroccan cushions.

"Where were you when Fatima collapsed?" Benali's pen hovered over his notebook.

"I was in the garden, feeding that sweet orange tabby." Edith adjusted her red-framed glasses. "Though I can't find my reading glasses anywhere. The stress of all this is making me terribly scattered."

"They are on your nose. And you were feeding a cat. Of course. Did you see anything unusual?"

"Oh!" She put a hand to her face and shook her head. "I'd lose my eyeballs themselves if they ever fell out of their sockets. And yes, actually. I saw Fatima stumble in through the front entrance. She looked quite ill." Edith's hands fluttered like nervous birds. "I called out to her, but she didn't respond. I assumed she couldn't hear me over the fountain. Amira came in with her, and then, a moment later, Amira shouted."

Benali made a note. "Amira came in with her? Do you mean Amira el-Fasi, the fortune teller? What time was this?"

"Yes, that's the one." Edith nodded. "And it was just after four. I'd just finished my afternoon tea."

Emma shifted her weight, noting how Benali's expression sharpened at the mention of Amira.

When he'd finished jotting this down, Benali looked around the salon. He said something in Arabic, and Khadija ran to the kitchen, returning a moment later with Amira.

Amira glided into the chair, her silver bracelets catching the light. Her dark eyes met Benali's steadily.

There was a conversation in Arabic, and Emma wished she had somehow become fluent in
144

the language overnight. As it was, so only understood one word.

"*La*." Amira's hands remained folded in her lap. It meant 'no,' and the fortune teller's gaze was steady as she said it.

Benali sighed and asked for Derek.

Derek slouched down the stairs, hands jammed in his pockets. His eyes looked tired, and he appeared not to know what had happened. "I already told you everything about Ruby and me."

"And now I'm asking about Fatima," Benali said sharply. "Where were you this afternoon?"

"Fatima?" Derek looked around the salon. "Did you find her?"

Benali nodded. "Indeed. We found her unconscious on the ground, right over there."

Derek gaped. "You- what?" He sat up straighter and looked where Benali had pointed. "Wait. Was that the sirens?"

Benali nodded dryly and asked again, "And I repeat. Where were you this afternoon?"

Derek stared at him. "Is she…"

Benali took a slow breath. "Fatima is not dead. Yet. But she is not well. And where were you, Mr. Astor?"

"Business center earlier. Then my room." He shook his head before being asked. "No witnesses. I was alone."

As Victor's turn approached, Emma touched Khadija's arm. The girl had been hovering near the

145

kitchen entrance, watching everything with wide
eyes.

"Khadija," Emma whispered, motioning her
into the stairwell. "I need your help. Victor asked
me to get something from his room while he talks to
the detective."

Khadija's brow furrowed. "But Mr. Victor
did not say-"

Emma met her eyes and hesitated. "Ok.
You're right. But please trust me. I'm trying to help
find out what happened to Ruby and Fatima."

Khadija bit her lip, then nodded slowly and
glanced into the salon. She led Emma up the stairs
while Benali's voice drifted after them.

"Mr. Novikov, you were where this
afternoon?"

"Upstairs," Emma heard him say.
"Reading."

Emma followed Khadija down the hall, their
footsteps muffled by the thick carpet runner. The
young girl produced a key ring and unlocked
Victor's door with practiced efficiency.

"I will wait here," Khadija whispered,
staying in the hallway.

Emma gave her a grateful nod and slipped
inside, heart pounding. Victor's room was neat, with
his suitcase tucked in the corner. A laptop sat closed
on the desk. She had no idea what she was looking
for. Evidence? Something to connect Victor to

Ruby in the Seychelles ten years ago? Perhaps a vial of poison?

Below, she could still hear the murmur of voices as Benali continued his interviews.

Emma moved as silently as she could, conscious of every sound. She pulled open the desk drawer - nothing but hotel stationery and a pen. She flipped open the laptop, but it was password protected.

The nightstand held a paperback novel in Russian, an English copy of *An American Tragedy*, by a Theodore Dreiser, and a half-empty water glass. She checked under the pillow, finding only the cool cotton of the pillowcase.

In the closet, shirts hung neatly pressed. Emma ran her hands through the pockets of a navy blazer, finding only a crumpled receipt from a café. A dusty duffle bag sat on the closet floor, containing dirty clothes from his desert trip.

The bathroom counter held basic toiletries - toothbrush, razor, deodorant. Emma opened the medicine cabinet, seeing only aspirin and bandages.

She returned to the main room just as Khadija poked her head in the door and whispered, "Someone is coming, Miss Emma."

Emma spotted a pair of slacks over the arm of a small couch. Hurrying over, she checked the pockets and sucked in her breath.

A leather wallet. Her fingers trembled and she glanced toward the door as she pulled it out.

147

A few credit cards. Some cash. An old newspaper clipping, folded multiple times. Emma carefully unfolded it, revealing an article in Russian.

"Hurry," Khadija said.

Emma returned the article and felt something else- a back flap.

Her fingers trembled as she lifted it.

A folded photo slipped out. Her breath caught.

A younger Victor, tanned and smiling, stood on a white sand beach, his arm around a happy Ruby. Crystal-clear waters and towering palm trees framed them. Ruby's smile was radiant.

As footsteps sounded in the hall, Emma pulled out her phone and snapped a photo of the image.

As she shoved it back in the compartment, she felt a paper.

Folded once, with an address scrawled in blue ink.

She snapped a photo and slid it back, shoving the wallet into the pants pocket.

"You should perhaps clean that mud from your shoes, Miss Edith," Khadija said in the hall, "before you come any further in the hall, please."

Emma arranged the slacks as neatly as she could with shaking hands before slipping to the doorway.

Khadija let out a breath of relief. "I sent Miss Edith back downstairs," she whispered. "To give you time."

Emma gave the girl a quick hug. "*Shukran*."

The young girl nodded, dark eyes serious as she locked the door. "Did you find what you needed?"

Emma touched the phone in her pocket. "I think I found more than I expected."

Emma's mind raced as she made her steps go slowly along the hall.

The handwriting on that paper was familiar. She'd seen it before.

The notebook.

In her room, she pulled out her phone and looked at the two photos she'd taken. Then she scrolled back to the photos of the notebook pages.

She was right. There were the same sharp angles on the letters, the same distinctive way of writing the number four.

Victor.

She thought back to that first dinner. Victor had kept shifting his chair, ducking behind the potted palm. He'd told Daniel he didn't like groups. But was it possible that he shifted whenever Ruby glanced his way? At the time, Emma had written it off as odd behavior, but now...

"Oh my gosh. He was hiding from her," Emma whispered. "Stalking her! He didn't want her to recognize him."

But Victor had been in the Sahara when Ruby died. Hadn't he? Emma remembered his claims about the expensive hotel being a strain on his limited budget. Yet he'd kept his room even while supposedly away in the desert.

What if he hadn't gone at all?

But something still didn't add up. If Victor had killed Ruby, why was Fatima now poisoned too? Were the two incidents connected? And if Victor was involved, how had he managed to poison Ruby while supposedly away in the desert?

Chapter 17

Emma slipped back into the salon, heart still racing from her discoveries in Victor's room. The familiar scent of mint tea mingled with something sharper - whiskey, she guessed, noting the amber liquid in Dr. Grant's glass.

Benali stood near the archway leading to the kitchen, speaking in low tones with Dresia. The cook's usual commanding presence seemed diminished, her shoulders tight as she answered the detective's questions.

Daniel caught Emma's eye from across the room and raised his eyebrows in question. She gave a slight shake of her head, glancing to Victor lounging on the couch just beyond Daniel's shoulder. Victor raised his own glass in a mock toast to Dr. Grant, who barely acknowledged the gesture. Edith Pimm perched between them on an embroidered ottoman. Her hand shook as she petted the stray orange cat on her lap.

Emma's gaze drifted to the far corner where Brian slumped in an armchair, his face ashen. Derek sat rigid beside him, while Adeline paced behind their chairs. Emma's phone felt heavy in her pocket, the photos of Victor's wallet contents nearly burning against her hip.

Benali's voice carried across the room, his Arabic sounding harsh.

Dresia nodded and answered in a quiet voice.

Emma glanced at Victor, but his face remained impassive as he sipped his drink. Nothing in his manner suggested he'd been stalking Ruby or had any connection to her death or Fatima's collapse. And yet that photo...

Daniel shifted in his seat, clearly wanting to ask Emma where she'd disappeared to, but she kept her eyes fixed on Benali's conversation with Dresia. Now wasn't the time to share what she'd found - not with Victor sitting right there, close enough that she could smell his cologne.

Emma edged away from the salon.

In the entry, Mustafa stood organizing papers at the front desk. The sound of voices from the salon drifted down the hall - Benali's louder tones mixing with Dresia's responses in Arabic.

"Mustafa," Emma kept her voice low. "I need to ask you something about Victor."

He looked up. "Of course."

"The night he left for his desert trip - you saw him go?"

"Yes, just after dinner that first night." Mustafa straightened a stack of papers. "He had his bag packed and everything."

Emma nodded, remembering. She had seen him leave as well. "And you saw him return the next day?"

"Yes, covered in dust from the desert."
Mustafa's brow furrowed. "Why do you ask?"

Emma glanced back toward the salon. "I
was wondering - is there any way to verify that he
actually went to the desert? Could he have stayed in
Marrakesh instead?"

"Ah." Mustafa's eyes widened slightly. "You
think perhaps..." He trailed off, then pulled out his
phone. "I can call Mohammed Sidiqi. He arranges
all the desert expeditions. He will know if Mr.
Novikov was truly there."

Emma nodded, slightly amused that there
was another Mohammed. "Would you? Please?"

Mustafa dialed and spoke rapidly in Arabic.
Emma caught only a word here and there - "Sahara"
and what she thought might be Victor's name. After
a brief exchange, Mustafa hung up.

"Mohammed will come here," Mustafa said.
"He says it is better to discuss in person. He will be
here very soon."

"Thank you." Emma held his gaze. "Please
don't mention this to anyone else yet?"

"Of course not." Mustafa's expression grew
serious. "You think Mr. Novikov might be involved
in what happened to Mrs. Astor?"

"I'm not sure yet," Emma said. "But I want
to know if he could have been in town."

From the salon, she heard Daniel call her
name.

"I should get back," she said. "But please let me know the moment Mohammed Sidiqi arrives?"

Mustafa nodded, and Emma slipped back toward the salon. If Victor hadn't actually gone to the desert, it might explain how Ruby had died. But it still didn't explain Fatima's collapse.

Emma sat beside Daniel in the salon, her fingers drumming against the arm of her chair. The sweet scent of honey and sesame came from a plate of fresh sh'bakia Dresia had set on the low table. But Emma's stomach twisted - her appetite had vanished.

Victor lounged across from them, still nursing his drink. Every few minutes, Emma caught herself staring at him and had to blink and look away. Had he been following Ruby all these years? Questions crowded her mind, making it impossible to focus on the quiet conversations around her.

Movement caught her eye. From the doorway, Mustafa gave her a subtle nod.

"I'll be right back," she murmured to Daniel, rising from her seat.

But as she stepped into the lobby, Emma froze. The man standing with Mustafa was instantly familiar - the same man she'd watched Daniel speaking with in the medina earlier. Her confusion lasted only a moment before understanding hit her like a physical blow.

Daniel had already been checking Victor's alibi. Without telling her.

154

The hurt pierced deep, followed quickly by anger. After everything they'd been through together solving cases, after he'd said he wasn't investigating without her and that he would explain, he was still keeping her in the dark.

Emma took a deep breath, forcing herself to focus. Her feelings about Daniel's secretiveness would have to wait. Right now, she needed to know about Victor's supposed desert trip.

"*S'lema*," she said carefully to Mohammed, using one of the new Arabic words she'd learned.

Mustafa gestured to Emma and said something to Mohammed in rapid Arabic.

Mohammed's eyes darted around the entry, appearing nervous.

"Perhaps we should speak somewhere more private?" Mustafa said.

"Yes, of course." Emma nodded.

Mustafa led them down a short hallway to a small room furnished with a wooden desk and chairs.

Emma tried out one of the Arabic phrases she'd been practicing. "*Shukran* for coming to speak with me."

Mohammed nodded. "Of course." He still looked worried. Did he guess, Emma wondered, what she was about to ask him? Was he in on Victor's deception, afraid that he was about to have to lie to her, and perhaps to the police?

"My English is not good," he said, worry clear in his eyes.

"Ah." Emma pulled out her phone and opened her translator app. "It's okay. I'm still learning. I only know a couple of Arabic words."

Mohammed perched on the edge of his chair, his fingers drumming nervously against his knee.

Emma typed into her phone. "I have a question about a client of yours."

Now Mohammed looked positively alarmed. He glanced at the door, then looked to Mustafa as if begging for help. But Mustafa shook his head and said something in Arabic. Emma clearly caught the name Victor Novikov. At that, Mohammed relaxed, and his face broke into a smile. He and Mustafa exchanged a few more words in Arabis and both men laughed.

Emma was bewildered. "What?" she asked. "Why is this funny?"

"No," Mustafa said. "Not funny, of course." But the two men shared another smile, and Emma knew there was something they found amusing that they weren't telling her.

Exasperated, she typed, "Was Victor Novikov in the desert with you five nights ago? He was supposed to be on your desert expedition."

Mohammed smiled. "Yes, the Russian journalist. He was in the desert that night and he was, how do you say it... enthusiastic about the trip."

Emma's heart sank. "He was definitely there? The whole time?"

Mohammed nodded. "Oh yes. He took many photos of the sunset and sunrise."

Mohammed mimed a phone taking photos and said, "He liked camel ride, though he was, how do you say?" He patted his thighs and said something in Arabic.

"Sore," Mustafa translated, and Mohammed nodded.

"I see." Emma felt deflated. If Victor had truly been in the desert, how could he have killed Ruby? "And you're certain he stayed the entire night?"

Mohammed nodded as he answered. "*Na'am*. Yes," Mustafa said. "We had mint tea around the fire, and he slept in one of the Bedouin tents."

Emma looked at his face. He still carried a happy, almost relieved expression. She forced a smile. "*Shukran*." She glanced toward the door, remembering that Daniel had spoken with this same man yesterday. "When you talked with Detective Lindberg about this..."

Mustafa held up a hand and translated her words into Arabic. Both men both shook their heads. "He has not spoken with your Detective Lindberg," Mustafa said.

Mohammed stood, giving Emma a questioning look. Even without translation, she could tell he was asking if that was all.

Emma nodded, confused that he was lying about talking to Daniel. She'd seen them talking. Surely he knew that. "Thank you for your time. I mean, *shukran*."

After Mohammed left, Emma lingered in Mustafa's office, trying to make sense of it all. Why had he lied about seeing Daniel. And was he also lying about Victor going to the desert? He'd appeared relieved to talk about Victor.

Victor, who had an old photo of Ruby and detailed notes about her movements - now appeared to have a solid alibi for the night of her death.

What was going on?

The sound of Daniel's voice in the entry snapped her from her thoughts. "Emma? Are you back here?"

She stepped into the hallway, meeting his concerned gaze. "We need to talk."

"Just a moment, Mr. Lindberg, if you please. I have a question about your bill," Mustafa said.

"Of course." Daniel gave Emma an apologetic look. "One minute?"

Emma sat alone in the salon, cradling a glass of mint tea between her palms. The sweet scent wafted up, mingling with the aroma of oranges from the riad garden and the lingering scent of Dr. Grant's whiskey. Everyone else had retreated to
158

their rooms after Benali's questioning, leaving her with only her troubled thoughts for company.

She pulled her journal from her bag and flipped it open. A blank page stared back at her. She clicked her pen and began writing everyone's names, sketching a link chart, drawing circles and connecting them with lines.

"Ruby," she murmured, writing the name. She drew lines branching out to other circles - Derek, Brian, Fatima, Victor, Adeline.

She tapped her pen against the paper. Fatima was unconscious in the hospital after collapsing in this very room. She had argued with Ruby and was having an affair with Brian. Emma added that detail in small text along the connecting line.

"Victor..." She traced the line to his name. The photo in his wallet showed him with Ruby in the Seychelles a decade ago, three years before she married Derek. Yet Victor had been in the desert when Ruby died - Mohammed had confirmed that.

She drew a dotted line between Derek and Ruby, writing "estranged but reconciling?" beside it. The necklace he'd given her as a wedding gift had turned up in the trash. Why did someone stage a theft only to dispose of it? Surely it could have been sold.

She wrote in Edith, Dr. Grant, Dresia, Mina, Mustafa- and even Khadija- although she could see no way any of them were connected.

"And then there's Amira," Emma muttered, adding another circle. How had the fortune teller known about the threatening note? She connected Amira to Ruby with a question mark. And Amira come into the hotel with Fatima right before Fatima collapsed. Surely that wasn't a coincidence. But how was Amira connected to any of them?

Shaking her head in confusion, she drew connecting lines from Amira to both Ruby and Fatima and labeled them 'fortune,' and 'arrival.'

The lines formed a web across the page, but the center kept drawing her eye back to Brian. He was the most closely connected to both Ruby and Fatima. Plus, she'd seen him with Fatima near Zahra's shop, in the area of the city where magic potions and deadly poisons were sold.

"Could a father really..." Emma couldn't finish the thought aloud. But she wrote it anyway: "Brian killed Ruby? Or plotted with Fatima?"

It made a horrible kind of sense. If Fatima had fled after helping kill Ruby, Brian's silence would have been protecting her. And he hadn't told Benali where she lived. But when she returned - was he worried she'd confess? Implicate him?

Emma drew a line between Derek and Fatima, noting "father-in-law's mistress" beside it. Another potential connection, but was it a possible motive?

She sat back, studying the diagram. The lines twisted and intersected like the narrow streets
160

of the medina. But something still felt off. She circled Victor's name again, staring at it.

"Why keep photos and take notes about Ruby?" she whispered. "And what about the notebook? What am I missing?"

The sound of Daniel's footsteps returning made her close her journal quickly. She wasn't ready to share her thoughts with him yet - not when he was keeping his own investigation secret from her.

She had just slipped her notebook back into her bag when Daniel strode into the salon. His face was flushed with excitement as he bent to give her a quick kiss.

"I need to run a quick errand. Won't be long."

Emma's fingers tightened around her tea glass. "Another mysterious errand? Daniel, what's going on?"

"I promise I'll tell you everything soon." He squeezed her shoulder and smiled at her. "Trust me?"

"That's not fair." She pulled away from his touch. "We're supposed to be partners in this. Remember Paris? Venice? The cases back home? What changed?"

Daniel grinned at her. "Nothing's changed. I just need to confirm something first. Give me an hour?"

"Fine." Emma crossed her arms. Despite her frustration, it was hard to be angry with him when he smiled at her like that.

He bent to give her another kiss, then turned and left. Emma watched him disappear through the arched doorway, her frustration building as the sound of his footsteps faded down the corridor.

She pulled her phone from her pocket and opened the photo of the slip of paper. "Well," she muttered, "I might as well go do some investigating of my own."

She typed the address into her phone's map app. It wasn't far - just a few blocks into the medina. Emma gathered her things, making sure to tuck her journal safely away in her bag.

Mustafa stood at his desk in the front lobby. "Everything is okay, Ms. Harper?"

"Yes, thank you." She smiled. "I'm going to take a walk, clear my head after all the excitement."

"Have a nice time. Maybe some shopping. But do be careful. We don't need any more accidents."

"I won't be long," Emma promised, already heading for the door. She had an hour before Daniel returned- plenty of time to check out this address and be back before he returned from his own mysterious errand.

Chapter 18

Emma stepped out of the hotel into the warm evening air. The sun had begun to set, painting the ochre walls of the medina in deep orange and purple shadows. She pulled up the photo of the address on her phone, then re-opened her map app.

The streets were still busy with locals heading home and tourists searching for dinner spots. Emma wove between two elderly Moroccan women carrying wooden boards piled with bread and a group of children kicking a soccer ball.

"*Shukran*," she called out as she squeezed past a cart seller, proud to use one of the few Arabic words she'd mastered.

The man smiled and nodded, continuing his calls advertising fresh dates and nuts.

The street grew darker as the buildings pressed closer together. The smells of dinner cooking - cumin, garlic, preserved lemons - wafted from hidden courtyards.

Her phone buzzed with a new direction, and she turned left down a narrower alley. The sounds of the main street faded, replaced by the soft echo of her footsteps on ancient stones. A cat darted across her path, disappearing into a doorway. She entered the covered part of the market, where fabric had been draped over the walkways to provide shade during the heat of the day. Now, it was notably darker in this section of the medina.

"Okay, next right," she muttered, following the blue line on her screen. The alley twisted and turned, each corner revealing another stretch of tiny shops and wooden doors.

Emma paused at an intersection, double-checking the route. A group of teenage boys lounged nearby, and one called out "*Bonjour!*" She smiled and nodded but kept walking. The tiny shops were looking familiar. She'd been here before.

Her phone indicated she was getting close. Just one more turn and...

Emma stopped short. "Oh, no."

But there it was - Zahra's shop, exactly where Victor's mysterious address had led her. The same wooden shelves lined with glass jars of dried plants and powders. The same strings of garlic, dried peppers, and mysterious dead lizards hanging from the ceiling.

A chill ran down her spine despite the lingering heat of the day.

Emma took a step back, suddenly very aware of how dark it had gotten.

"Ok. Now that I know, time to head back," she whispered to herself, already turning to retrace her steps when Zahra emerged from the back of the shop.

"Emma! We meet again!"

Emma hesitated, then stepped toward Zahra's tiny shop. Bundles of dried flowers hung from the ceiling - lavender, chamomile, and others she couldn't identify. Glass jars lined wooden shelves, filled with powders, roots, and dried leaves. A desiccated toad lay on its back next to what appeared to be snake skins.

"It is wonderful to see you," Zahra said with a smile.

"*S'lema*, Zahra," Emma said, running her finger along a shelf of clay pots. "It's good to see you too." She glanced around. "Your shop is fascinating. Do you get many foreign customers?"

"Some tourists, yes. They buy safer herbs - mint for tea, saffron for cooking." Zahra adjusted a string of small lizards hanging near the door.

"Has a Russian man named Victor been in recently?"

"Russian man? No, I don't think so." Zahra moved behind her wooden counter, straightening jars of dried rose petals.

Emma bit her lip, glancing at the photo on her phone. "What about an American businessman, Brian Johnson? Or his assistant Fatima?"

"No, I haven't seen the American man. But Fatima?" Zahra picked up a dried scorpion and placed it in a glass case. "That is a very common Moroccan name." She smiled. "I have many customers named Fatima."

"Oh, of course," Emma said. "How about a Derek Astor?"

"No, none of these people have been to my shop." Zahra's dark eyes studied Emma. "You are asking about the woman who died?"

Emma nodded. "The police said it was blue thistle poison. As you know."

"Ah yes, in Arabic we call it *addad*. A dangerous plant." Zahra reached under the counter and pulled out a dried specimen with spiky purple flowers. "Very poisonous if not prepared correctly."

"How would someone use it as a poison?"

"There are many ways. It can be made into a powder, added to food or drink." Zahra carefully returned the plant to its drawer. "Tea could be used - mint would likely mask the bitter taste."

Emma thought of the shattered tea service in Ruby's room. "But you're certain none of the hotel guests bought any?"

"No, I did not see any of them come here. I would remember selling *addad*."

Emma pulled up the photo on her phone. "What about this address? It is for your shop, right?"

Zahra examined the screen. "Yes, that's my address. But I haven't seen any of the people you mention."

"Thank you," Emma sighed.

The beaded curtain at the back of the shop rattled and a tall young man entered, carrying a cloth bag.

"Ah, Ahmed! Did you get everything?" Zahra asked. To Emma she added, "This is my assistant, Ahmed."

"*Na'am*. All the supplies you needed." He set the bag on the counter, sending a small cloud of dust into the air. He smiled at Emma.

"*S'lema*," she said.

The young man beamed and replied in a string of Arabic.

Emma shook her head. "That's about all my Arabic," she said with a smile. "*La, shukran, s'lema, sh'bakia*… and now *addad*. Oh, and *en'sha Allah*." A thought struck her. "Ahmed, you are Zahra's assistant. Have you sold any *addad* recently? To any foreigners?"

His face brightened. "Yes! Last week - an American doctor from the embassy bought some roots."

Emma's breath caught. "Dr. Grant?"

Chapter 19

"I didn't want to sell it to him," Ahmed said, unpacking dried flowers from his bag. "It's very dangerous, *addad*. But he showed his embassy ID and explained a project at the embassy."

Zahra stared at Ahmed and said something in Arabic. The young man shrugged and raised his hands.

"Well," Zahra said to Emma. "Someone from the hotel has been here then."

Emma watched as Ahmed continued unpacking his supplies, her mind a whirl.

"A presentation for embassy staff?" Emma asked.

"Yes, yes." Ahmed nodded enthusiastically. "Dr. Grant said they need to know which plants are dangerous. For their children, you know? Many Americans come to Morocco and don't understand our plants."

Ahmed moved about the shop, methodically arranging dried flowers and roots in their proper places. The scents of cardamom, cinnamon, and unfamiliar spices filled the air.

A presentation about dangerous plants? Emma watched Ahmed stack jars. Any doctor could give that talk with photos or diagrams. Why would Dr. Grant need the actual poison?

Zahra pulled a bundle of dried lavender from Ahmed's bag and hung it from a hook in the ceiling. The motion stirred the air, sending dust motes dancing in the last rays of sunlight filtering through the shop's small window.

But maybe she was jumping to conclusions. Emma's gaze drifted to the doorway where she'd seen Brian and Fatima pass by that day. There had to be other shops selling *addad* in the medina. The twisted alleyways probably held dozens of herbalists and traditional medicine sellers.

Ahmed hummed as he worked, speaking occasionally to Zahra in Arabic. Emma leaned against the counter, remembering how jumpy Dr. Grant had been lately. But anyone could have taken the plant from him - if they'd known he had it.

Her memory caught on the slip of paper with Zahra's address. Victor may have gotten the address from another guest at the hotel. Maybe it wasn't Victor's handwriting at all. Maybe Dr. Grant had jotted the address down for him. In which case, the notebook would be Dr. Grant's. But then, why would Victor keep the paper hidden in his wallet with the photo of Ruby?

A thin white cat wandered in and wound between Emma's ankles, purring.

Dr. Grant's purchase could be innocent. Fatima and Brian's presence in this area might mean nothing. Victor's address might be unrelated.

But someone poisoned Ruby. And now possibly Fatima.

"When exactly did he buy the *addad*?"

"Last week. Tuesday, I think." Ahmed glanced at Zahra. "Or Wednesday? When were you out?"

"Tuesday," Zahra confirmed. "It was market day."

Emma opened her mouth to ask about Victor again, thinking perhaps Ahmed had seen him, but her phone buzzed in her pocket. Daniel's name lit up the screen.

"Fatima's awake," Daniel said. "Meet me at the hospital? She's in room 2033."

"Oh my gosh. Yes! I'll be right there." Emma ended the call and turned back to Zahra and Ahmed. "Thank you both. But I need to go!"

"*S'lema!*" Zahra said with a wave toward the door.

Chapter 20

Emma's footsteps echoed through the dimly lit hospital corridor. The antiseptic smell reminded her of hospitals back home, though the signs on the walls were in Arabic and French.

A nurse in a pale blue hijab looked up from her computer at the nurses' station. "Can I help you?"

"Room 2033? Fatima Alaoui?"

The nurse pointed down the hallway. "Third door on the right. But she's sleeping now. She woke briefly earlier."

"Thank you." Emma walked past rooms where medical equipment beeped steadily. Most doors were closed, with only a few rooms showing soft light from within.

She found 2033 and paused in the doorway. Fatima lay still beneath crisp white sheets, an IV dripping steadily beside her. The room was spare - just a bed, two chairs, a row of cupboards, and monitoring equipment casting a blue glow in the semi-darkness.

Footsteps approached behind her. Emma turned, expecting Daniel, but Dr. Grant stepped into the fluorescent light of the doorway, slightly out of breath, his bag slung over one shoulder.

Her stomach clenched as she saw him. "Dr. Grant? What brings you here?"

He blinked. "Word reached the hotel that she'd regained consciousness. I came to check on her condition." He glanced at his watch. "Brian should be here soon."

Emma moved closer to Fatima's bed, deliberately positioning herself between the sleeping woman and Dr. Grant. She couldn't see any way he was connected to the two women, but he had apparently bought *addad*. So she couldn't be too careful. "I got the news from Daniel. Are you sure someone told Brian? It seems like he would have been the first one here."

Dr. Grant nodded and glanced over his shoulder. "It does. I wonder if anyone actually told him." He took a step toward Fatima, a concerned look on his face, and gestured toward the door. "Perhaps you could run back and get him? I know he would want to be here. And the hospital can be confusing to navigate."

Emma didn't move. "I'll wait for Daniel. He should be here any minute."

"Really, I can stay with her." Dr. Grant stepped further into the room. "I'm a doctor. And the staff seems to have gone home for the night."

Emma remained firmly planted by the bed. "I promised Daniel I'd meet him here."

Dr. Grant smiled. "It's ok. Daniel will wait for you. I assure you Fatima will be in good hands."

"Of course." Emma forced a smile while her heart raced. Where was Daniel? "But I'd hate to miss Daniel. And visiting hours must be nearly over."

The monitoring equipment beeped steadily. Dr. Grant moved toward the IV stand, and Emma shifted to keep herself between him and Fatima.

"Ms. Harper..." He sounded confused. "You're acting like something's wrong. This is good news! Fatima woke up. Please, go let Brian know."

"No thank you." Emma met his gaze. "I'm staying right here until Daniel arrives."

They stood in uncomfortable silence, the fluorescent lights humming overhead. Emma counted each steady beep of the heart monitor, willing Daniel to hurry, when she heard Fatima's voice behind her whisper, "Emma?"

Emma turned as Fatima's eyes fluttered. The woman's usually immaculate appearance was disheveled, her dark hair tangled against the white hospital pillow.

"Emma?" Fatima's voice was barely a whisper. "Is that you?"

Dr. Grant stepped forward. "Please, she needs rest-"

Emma ignored him. "Fatima, how are you?"

Fatima's hand trembled as she reached for the bed rail. "I have been better."

Emma gave a weak smile. "I see that. Would you like some water?"

Fatima closed her eyes. "*La,*" she said so quietly Emma wasn't sure she'd said it at all.

175

"What happened?" Emma asked.

"I came... came back to find Brian. When I heard about Ruby..." Her voice cracked. "Is it true?"

Emma's throat tightened. "Yes. I'm so sorry."

Tears slid down Fatima's cheeks and onto her pillow. "*La!*. No, no, no..."

"Ms. Harper." Dr. Grant's voice was sharp. "You're upsetting her. Her body is under enough stress. This isn't helpful."

"Brian." Fatima's fingers clutched at the sheets. "I need Brian."

"See?" Dr. Grant gestured toward the door. "Go get him. That's what she needs right now."

Emma shook her head, keeping her eyes on Fatima. "Please, Fatima, can you tell me what happened when you came back to the hotel?"

"She needs to rest." Dr. Grant raised his voice and moved closer to the IV stand. "This questioning can wait."

"I saw..." Fatima's voice was growing weaker. "Victor. Outside hotel."

Emma leaned in. "Victor was there?"

"Offered me water... tasted strange." Fatima's eyes began to close. "That's all I..."

Outside the hotel. Where she'd found the necklace!

"Was he by the trash dumpster?" Emma asked quickly.

But Fatima's energy was spent. Her lips barely moved as she whispered, "Brian... please..."

Emma pulled out her phone, keeping one eye on Dr. Grant as he paced the length of the small hospital room from window to door, window to door.

She pressed Daniel's number. The phone rang three times before he picked up.

"Daniel? Are you and Brian on your way?"

"Just about to leaving the hotel. We ran into some issues. Everything okay?"

"Just get here soon." Emma watched Dr. Grant tug at his collar. "Please."

She ended the call and looked at Fatima. Victor had given her water, and it tasted strange. But Dr. Grant had been the one to buy the blue thistle. Had Victor stollen it from him?

Emma squared her shoulders and looked up. There was no time like the present. "Dr. Grant, why did you buy blue thistle from Zahra's shop?"

He stopped mid-stride. "What?"

"Her assistant confirmed you bought it last week."

"Who is Zahra? I don't know what you're talking about."

"She owns a shop in the medina. She sells medicinal plants. Her assistant is a tall young man, Ahmed."

When Dr. Grant didn't answer, Emma said, "Ahmed said you showed your embassy ID. Why did you buy it?"

"That's- that's not-" His hand trembled slightly as he adjusted his collar again. "I don't know what you're talking about."

"You told him it was for a presentation at the embassy about poisonous plants."

"No, I never-" He yanked at his tie, loosening it. "You can't possibly-"

"Then explain it to me."

"I can't." His voice cracked. "I can't say anything about it. You don't understand-"

The door swung open. Emma turned, relieved and expecting to see Daniel and Brain.

But her mouth fell open as Victor strode in wearing a white lab coat, a stethoscope draped around his neck. He froze when he saw her.

"What are you doing here?" They both asked at the same time.

Victor's pale green eyes darted from Emma to Dr. Grant, then to the sleeping Fatima. There was a beat of silence.

Then, quietly, he shut the door behind him.

Chapter 21

Emma's heart pounded as she stared at Victor in a lab coat. "Why are you dressed like a doctor? You're a journalist."

Dr. Grant's face drained of color. He backed away from Fatima's bed, nearly stumbling into the window ledge.

"I informed the nurse at the desk that I need privacy with my patient." Victor's accent seemed thicker now, his words precise. "No interruptions."

"Your patient?" Emma kept her voice steady despite the fear clawing at her throat. "You're not a doctor."

Emma glanced from Victor to Fatima, who lay still in the narrow bed, eyes closed, her chest rising and falling in shallow breaths. The steady beep of her heart monitor sounded oddly loud in the otherwise silent room. There was a red 'nurse call' button on a remote beside Fatima. Emma took a step toward it.

Victor's pale green eyes fixed on her with that unsettling intensity she'd noticed that first night at dinner. "You ask so many questions, Ms. Harper." He smiled as he put his hand into his lab coat pocket, and Emma saw something- a water bottle, perhaps, in the white pocket. "My travels. The Seychelles. Everyone's personal business. You are so nosey."

She swallowed, willing Daniel to burst through the door with Brian. The corridor beyond remained silent. Emma was acutely aware of how isolated this section of the hospital felt. No footsteps echoed in the hall, no voices carried through the walls. Just the soft beeping of machines and the quiet rhythm of Fatima's breathing.

Dr. Grant's hands were trembling. Sweat beaded on his forehead as he watched Victor's every move "Explain yourself." Dr. Grant's voice shook. "What are you doing here dressed like that? Did you do something to Fatima?"

Victor adjusted the stethoscope around his neck with careful precision. "Everyone plays a part in life, Dr. Grant. Like actors on a stage. Today, I needed access to this room."

"Parts?" Dr. Grant's face had gone red, sweat beading on his forehead. "This isn't some theater production!"

"Isn't it though?" Victor's smile didn't reach his eyes. "I played the poor journalist quite convincingly, didn't I? Even showed you my expired press credentials."

Emma's fingers inched toward her phone.

"I wouldn't do that if I were you, Ms. Harper." His voice was soft, almost gentle. "Put the phone down."

Emma set the phone on Fatima's bedside table. Again, her eyes darted to the nurse call button.

180

"Emma asked about the blue thistle!" Dr. Grant blurted out. "She talked to someone at a shop-"

"Blue thistle?" Victor's eyebrows rose. "What are you talking about?"

"The shop in the medina, I had to-" Dr. Grant's words tumbled out in a panicked rush.

"I think," Victor said, reaching back into his pocket, "we should all calm down and discuss this over some mint tea." He pulled out a green glass bottle.

Dr. Grant stumbled backward until he hit the wall. "No! Please!"

Chapter 22

Victor's smile turned cold as he set the green bottle on the bedside table. "I've put up with interfering women long enough in my life." He yanked open cabinet doors, searching through medical supplies. "And Ruby was the worst of them all."

Emma watched his movements, her mouth dry.

"We were perfect together in the Seychelles." Victor's voice softened with reminiscence. "The sunsets, the private dinners, the walks on the beach. I had found the woman of my dreams. I shared everything with her - my vision, my plans." He slammed another cabinet shut. "But she couldn't see the brilliance of it."

"What plans?" Emma's voice came out shakier than she expected.

Victor turned, his pale green eyes gleaming under the harsh hospital lights. "The manipulation of global markets, Ms. Harper. The ability to shape economies with just a few well-placed stories." He gestured expansively. "I had everything prepared - evidence of corporate misconduct, whistleblower testimonies, leaked documents. All it would take was one big exposé. It was in the final draft."

"Fabricated evidence," Emma said softly, understanding dawning.

"Creative evidence," Victor corrected. "Art, Ms. Harper. The art of moving billions of American dollars with words." He leaned against the cabinet. "They are like magic, written words. If you wave your fingers over a keyboard, hold out a few shiny pieces of creative evidence, people will believe anything. Especially if they already want to believe it."

He sighed. "But Ruby - sweet, self-righteous Ruby - thought she knew better. She gathered her own evidence. Of my methods, my sources, my drafts. All while she was spending her nights with me on those white sand beaches." His fingers drummed against the metal surface as he scanned the open cupboards looking for something. "Of course, I didn't know who she was. I didn't know her father owned one of the companies I was targeting."

Dr. Grant made a choked sound. "You were going to destroy Brian's company?"

"I didn't know who she was then." Victor waved his hand dismissively as he found what he was looking for. He took a few paper cups from a cupboard and set them beside the green bottle. "But she took everything - my reputation, my career, my future. Rejected me as her lover and released it all anonymously to the media." His lip curled. "As if I wouldn't know it was her. The timing was too perfect, the details too precise. I could almost smell

184

the sunscreen on her skin when I read what she released. I knew it was her."

"So you killed her?" Emma's voice shook. "Because she exposed your lies?"

"I eliminated a threat." Victor's voice remained calm, reasonable, as he gave a small shrug. "Do you know what it's like writing travel pieces about camel rides when you should be moving markets? When you had the power to shape global economies in your hands?" He picked up the green bottle and unscrewed the lid. "Ruby needed to understand there are consequences to destroying a man's life."

Victor held out the open bottle to Dr. Grant. "Time to finish what you started. Finish Fatima."

Emma's heart hammered. The green liquid sloshed inside the bottle.

"I won't." Dr. Grant's voice cracked.

"You bought the blue thistle." Victor's tone hardened as he stepped toward Dr. Grant. "You'll do this too. Or I'll let everyone at the embassy know about your affair with the honorable ambassador's wife, your dear Sylvia."

Emma lunged forward, her hand connecting with the bottle. Glass shattered. Liquid splashed across the counter and floor, covering Dr. Grant's face and hands.

Dr. Grant gasped, pawing at his skin. His knees buckled and he collapsed against the wall, sliding down to the floor.

"Unfortunate." Victor said casually, as if discussing a change in weather. "Blue thistle is quite toxic, even through the skin. He'll be dead within minutes."

Emma lunged toward Fatima's bed, diving for the nurse call button.

Victor dove after her, yanking the cord from the wall.

"No more interruptions." He grabbed her shoulders, shoving her face toward the puddle of spilled poison on the counter. "Join the good doctor, won't you?"

Emma twisted, bringing her knee up hard between his legs. Victor doubled over with a grunt of pain. She shoved past him across the room, yanking the door open. Her sandals slipped on the linoleum as she ran down the empty corridor.

"Help!" Her voice echoed off the sterile walls. "Somebody help!"

The nurses' station sat empty, papers scattered across the desk. A coffee cup still steamed.

Footsteps pounded behind her. Emma glanced back to see Victor running, stumbling, his face contorted with rage.

Looking wildly around, she saw a green exit sign at the end of the hall.

She tore forward, sandals slipping again, and slammed through the side exit.

Cold night air hit her face.

The street stretched dark and empty before her.

She didn't pause to look back. She just ran.

Chapter 23

The hospital's metal door clanged behind her.

Her sandals skidded on ancient cobblestones as she came to an intersection. Terracotta walls rose high on either side, blank except for a set of blue-painted doors set deep in arched alcoves.

Left or right? Her chest heaved. The alley stretched identical in both directions.

The hospital door banged again. Victor's footsteps echoed off stone.

She darted left, shoulder scraping rough plaster. The alley twisted, then forked. She took the right fork, then another left.

Her hand brushed her pocket, searching for her phone - but it was empty. It was back in Fatima's room.

An elderly woman bumped against the wall as Emma rounded another corner.

"Sorry!" Emma called.

The passage opened wider. Colored lights and voices spilled ahead. The Jemaa el-Fnaa.

She exploded into the square.

Night air was thick with smoke from food stalls. Drums pounded. A fire-eater spewed flames toward a star-filled sky.

"Help!" she tried to call, but her voice came out a breathless gasp.

She weaved through the crowd. Pushed past a snake charmer's circle where cobras swayed. Past carts piled with dates and figs. Bumped into a water man in a huge hat. Her lungs burned.

"Stop!" Victor's voice carried over the crowd. Too close. "Stop that woman!"

Tourists turned to stare. Emma ducked between two juice carts dripping with chains of orange peels. Her toe caught the edge of a carpet spread with trinkets. She stumbled, catching herself on a pole.

The merchant shouted as his wares scattered. Emma shoved the display over behind her. Metal bowls and brass lamps crashed across the cobblestones.

She spotted a gap between buildings - barely wider than her shoulders. Without slowing, she squeezed into the darkness.

Rough walls scraped her right arm. The alley kinked left, then right.

She pressed into a doorway, holding her breath.

Footsteps pounded past her hiding spot. A flash of Victor's lab coat in the dim light.

She pushed herself out of the doorway and ran the opposite direction.

But he heard her sandals slapping the ground and shouted her name.

Emma's feet pounded against ancient stones as she darted back down the narrow passage. The maze of the alleys wove endless around her, walls rising three stories high on either side, broken only by narrow stairways and closed wooden doors.

Behind her, Victor's footsteps echoed closer.

"Think," she gasped. "The police station is near the square."

But which direction? Every alley looked the same - weathered terracotta walls, doors set in arches, occasional strings of lights crossing overhead.

She'd passed that carved wooden door before, hadn't she?

She was running in circles.

A cat darted across her path.

Emma stumbled, catching herself against a wall. Her palm scraped rough plaster. She needed height, needed to see where she was going.

A metal staircase climbed the side of a building.

Emma grabbed the railing and took the steps two at a time. Metal clanged under her feet.

She burst onto the rooftop terrace and paused, gasping for breath.

The sight stopped her in her tracks.

Marrakesh spread before her like something from Arabian Nights. Domed mosques and slim minarets pierced the star-filled sky. Strings of lights crisscrossed the narrow streets below. The glow of the Jemaa el-Fnaa lit the night sky to her right.

And there - just past the square - stood the boxy modern police station with the Moroccan flag.

She looked over the edge and her vision tipped with the dizzying height. She put a hand on a satellite dish to steady herself.

"Yes!" Emma whispered, trying to quell her fear of heights and memorize the path through the city to the station. "Left at the wider road. If I can just-"

Metal rang against metal. Footsteps on the stairs.

Emma spun toward the sound.

Victor's head appeared above the edge of the roof. His face gleamed with sweat in the starlight. The white lab coat made him look ghostly.

"Nowhere left to run, Ms. Harper." His Russian accent was thick, his voice was calm. Although he was panting, he sounded almost conversational. He took another step up. "Though I do admire your determination."

Emma backed away, her eyes darting around the roof. No other exits. No other staircases. Just a satellite dish and potted plants throwing strange shadows in the moonlight.

And the drop off the roof that made her head swim.

"You really should have stayed out of this." Victor reached the top of the stairs. "But then, that
192

was Ruby's problem too, wasn't it? And Fatima's, now that I think about it. None of you women could mind your own business."

Chapter 24

Victor stepped closer, lab coat fluttering in the night breeze. "You could have had a nice vacation, gone home to your little bakery."

Emma's heel hit the low wall at the roof's edge. Her stomach lurched. Three stories down, the alley gaped in darkness.

"But no." Victor's pale eyes gleamed. "You had to play detective."

A string of lights swayed overhead, casting shifting shadows across the terrace. A prayer rug lay beside a water jug. The scent of jasmine was thick in the night air.

"Women." Victor shook his head. "Always trying to prove something. Women should stay home, be taken care of."

Emma's fingers found a small potted plant on the wall behind her.

"But no." Victor's lip curled. "You think you know better."

He lunged.

Emma hurled the pot.

Victor dodged.

Emma stepped onto the ledge. The gap between buildings yawned behind her - three feet of empty space over the alley. Her knees went weak. But Victor lunged again.

She jumped.

For one horrible moment she was suspended in air. Then her feet hit the neighboring roof. She stumbled, caught herself on her hands and knees.

Victor's curse echoed as he followed.

Emma's shoes slapped against concrete as she vaulted over a low wall between buildings. A satellite dish loomed - she ducked under it. Past drying laundry, around water tanks.

A metal table blocked her path. Emma grabbed it, tipped it over. It crashed behind her.

Victor swore in Russian.

Another gap between buildings. Emma leaped without slowing this time. Her ankle turned as she landed. She pushed up off her knees and ran faster.

The police station's lights beckoned in the distance. Just a few more rooftops.

A clothesline caught her shoulder. She slipped on someone's abandoned tea tray, a glass shattering.

Victor's footsteps grew closer.

Emma sprinted toward the next building - and skidded to a stop.

Her toes curled over the edge of a sheer drop. Below, a wide avenue stretched between her and the next building.

No more rooftops to jump to. No fire escapes. No stairs. Just straight down to the street.

Shaking, Emma backed away from the edge.

Victor's breathing came harsh behind her. "End of the line."

He pulled a plastic bag from his lab coat pocket. In the dim light of the moon, Emma made out something dark and twisted inside.

"Confused?" Victor's laugh echoed across the rooftop. "Would you like to see what's left of Dr. Grant's little purchase?"

The night air felt thick and hot. The tasseled edge of a prayer rug fluttered in the breeze beside an old metal table.

"Poor Jimmy." Victor shook his head. "He never planned any embassy presentation about poisonous plants. That was my idea - a favor, really. Help him save his career."

"What do you mean?" Emma gasped, trying to get her breath.

"Such a scandal it would have been. The embassy doctor spending a romantic weekend in Marrakesh with the ambassador's wife." Victor's smile widened. "Sylvia Smith has a weakness for doctors, I suppose. Jimmy Grant needed my help to keep it quiet."

Emma's gaze darted between Victor and the street below. The rooftop felt smaller with each step he took toward her.

"Blue thistle is easily disguised in mint tea. Jimmy took it to Ruby that night - to calm her nerves, he said." Victor's voice turned cold. "It calmed her, all right. But Fatima saw him bringing up the tea. She had a fight with Brian and left. If she'd stayed away, she'd be fine. But no, she had to come back."

The plastic bag crinkled as Victor opened it. "Do you know what's interesting about blue thistle? It's far more toxic without water or tea to dilute it." He pulled back the edge of the bag revealing a twisted root, careful not to touch it. "Just one taste is enough to silence someone. Forever."

Emma forced herself to look over the edge. The street stretched empty and dark below, except for one man and a donkey plodding along, pulling a cart piled with linens.

The height made her dizzy. Could she survive the fall?

Victor stepped closer.

She inched toward the edge.

The root was dark in his outstretched hand.

She couldn't breathe.

He lunged.

Emma rolled to the side and Victor's momentum carried him forward.

His lab coat flashed white, and he windmilled his arms as he fell, then disappeared over the edge.

A muffled thump and crash echoed up from the street as Victor landed in the cart of laundry.

Chapter 25

Emma leaned over the edge of the rooftop, her hands trembling against the warm stone. "Help! Police! Stop him!" Her voice cracked as she screamed into the night air.

The man with the donkey cart dropped his lead rope and grabbed Victor's lab coat as he thrashed in the pile of linens. The man's voice rang out in rapid Arabic, echoing off the buildings.

Doors creaked open along the street. People emerged from their homes, surrounding the cart and looking up at the rooftop where Emma was still shouting to stop him. Two men pulled Victor from the laundry and held his arms as he struggled.

Emma spun around, her heart still racing, and pounded her fist against the metal rooftop door. "Please! Someone help!"

The door opened with a groan of rusty hinges. A girl about twelve years old stood frozen, her dark eyes wide. She wore pink pajamas decorated with cartoon cats and clutched a plush rabbit to her chest.

"*Ana asfa*," Emma gasped, barely aware enough to be surprised that she remembered this Arabic phrase. I'm sorry.

The girl's mother appeared behind her, wrapping a shawl around her shoulders. She wore a long cotton nightgown, and her black hair hung loose around her face.

"*Ajee*," the woman said, beckoning Emma inside. Come here.

Emma followed them down narrow stairs into a home that smelled of mint and saffron. Copper lanterns cast warm light across tiles in intricate geometric patterns. A television played softly in the corner where a younger child slept on cushions, surrounded by scattered toy cars.

"*Shukran*," Emma whispered. Thank you.

The mother nodded and guided Emma through their small living room. Prayer beads hung beside family photos on the walls. A pot of mint tea sat cooling on a low table next to half-finished homework papers.

They reached the heavy wooden door that led to the street just as Detective Benali emerged from the shadows. He strode toward the group of men restraining Victor, his white hat gleaming under the streetlights.

"*S'lema. Shukran.*," Emma called back to the family as she rushed outside. Goodbye. Thank you.

The young girl stared after her from the doorway, still clutching her stuffed rabbit, as her mother drew her back inside and closed the door.

Chapter 26

Emma watched Dresia's hands shape the couscous into a perfect cone. Steam rose from the fluffy grains as Dresia decorated the sides with strips of caramelized onion, zucchini, and chickpeas.

"*Zwin*," Khadija said, nodding approval at Emma's attempt to copy Dresia's technique. Beautiful.

Emma's couscous listed slightly to one side, but she was pleased with her attempt. The kitchen was filled with the scent of saffron and preserved lemons as the chicken tagine bubbled in its clay pot.

The door swung open, and Mina bustled in wearing a light blue caftan. "*Sabah al-kheir*," she called out, tying an apron around her waist.

"Good morning to you too," Emma said, relieved to see Mina looking happy again. "Want to help with the *b'stilla*?"

"*Na'am*!" Mina's eyes lit up as she moved to the counter. Her fingers flew as she separated sheets of paper-thin dough.

"Mina is teaching me to make this at home," Khadija said with a smile.

Emma watched in amazement as Mina crafted perfect little folds in the dough, creating delicate patterns that would show through once baked. "You're incredible at this."

"*Shukran*." Mina's cheeks flushed with pleasure.

Khadija translated between them as they worked, her voice growing more confident with each exchange. The kitchen filled with laughter as Emma mangled another Arabic phrase.

"*La*, no," Khadija giggled, "*Zwin* means beautiful. You just said the tagine is a camel!"

The kitchen door opened again, and Daniel stepped in. His blue eyes found Emma's.

"Hey," he said softly. "Got a minute?"

Emma wiped her hands on her apron. "Of course. Everything okay?"

"The embassy Marines just came for Dr. Grant." Daniel leaned against the counter. "He's going to be okay - someone found him at the hospital, and they got him treatment in time. Apparently Victor saw Dr. Grant with Sylvia and recognized her as the ambassador's wife. He blackmailed Grant into buying the blue thistle, taking the tea up to Ruby, and faking the break in. Grant gave his full statement to Benali before the Marines took him. "

"Thank goodness." Emma let out a breath she hadn't realized she'd been holding. "And Victor?"

"Still denying everything, but it won't matter. Between your testimony, Grant's statement, and once Fatima's well enough to talk..." Daniel shook his head. "He's not getting out of this one."

"Good." Emma's hands trembled slightly as she reached for the honey to drizzle over the *sh'bakia*. "I keep thinking about what could have happened if-"

"Hey." Daniel caught her hands in his and pulled her into a hug "You're safe. It's over."

"And you'll get honey on your shirt," she said with a laugh.

Dresia called out something in Arabic and Khadija translated: "She says the tagine is ready!"

Emma smiled at Daniel and moved back to the stove. "Tell Dresia I won't let her chicken burn."

As she lifted the cone-shaped lid, the aroma of preserved lemons and olives filled the air. Emma smiled, watching Mina expertly crimping the edges of the *b'stilla* while Khadija sprinkled powdered sugar and cinnamon in intricate patterns across the top.

Half an hour later, Emma helped carry the steaming platters into the dining room where lantern light cast a warm glow over the gathered guests. Amazing smells filled the air as they set down the dishes.

Fatima sat beside Brian, her face pale but smiling as she leaned against his shoulder. Her hand trembled slightly as she reached for her water glass.

"Let me," Brian said softly, helping her take a sip.

203

Khadija flitted around the tables, refilling water glasses and setting down baskets of fresh bread. The young girl's face glowed with pride as the guests exclaimed over each dish.

"This couscous is magnificent," Edith declared, adjusting her bright red glasses. "Though I dare say not quite as spectacular as Fatima's recovery and finding out what really happened to poor Ruby."

Daniel set down his fork. "Grant finally broke down and told Benali everything. Victor had been planning this for years, tracking Ruby's movements, waiting for the right moment."

"But why?" Adeline asked, her green eyes bright with unshed tears. "What could Ruby possibly have done to deserve this?"

"She stopped him from destroying several companies, including mine," Brian's voice cracked. "She discovered his scheme to manipulate stock prices through false journalism. My own daughter saved my company, and I never even knew." He pressed his face into his hands.

Fatima rubbed his back gently. "She was protecting you, *habibi*."

"Grant admitted Victor blackmailed him into helping," Daniel continued. "He told Ruby the tea would help her sleep, knowing it was poisoned."

Derek pushed his plate away, his face ashen. "If we hadn't been fighting..."

"You couldn't have known," Adeline said softly. She brightened slightly. "Mohammed arrives tomorrow. We're coming together, to the funeral in the States."

Mustafa raised his glass. "To Ruby - may Allah grant her peace."

"To Ruby," they echoed.

Amira's bracelets clinked as she reached for her tea. "I saw darkness around her that night, but even I did not see this coming."

Emma watched the fortune teller take a sip of water. Could she really tell fortunes, Emma wondered?

Mina entered carrying a tray of *sh'bakia* and mint tea and smiled at Emma.

"Oh dear," Edith patted her pockets. "Has anyone seen my room key? I simply can't find it anywhere."

Mina's step faltered and her eyes widened, but Edith looked up and caught the look of fear on the young woman's face. Edith smiled warmly. "*Ajee*. Come sit beside me, Mina." Edith patted the spot on the low couch beside her. "I'll find my key somewhere. Things always turn up. Come share some tea and those lovely cookies you've got there."

Emma watched as Amira rose from her cushioned seat, her flowing caftan rustling as she crossed the room. The fortune teller's silver bracelets chimed with each graceful step.

To Emma's surprise, Amira settled beside her on the low couch. The older woman's dark eyes held Emma's gaze as she reached for Emma's hands. Emma glanced down at their joined hands, noticing how the intricate henna patterns on the backs of her own hands had begun to fade to a pale orange, while Amira's remained a deep brown.

"I am happy for you, child," Amira's melodic voice carried a warmth that made Emma's skin tingle.

"Thank you," Emma smiled. "I'm just glad we found out the truth about what happened to Ruby."

Amira's grip tightened slightly and her eyes crinkled. "That is good too. But no. No. That is not what I see." Her silver bangles caught the lantern light as she turned Emma's hand over and traced a finger along Emma's palm. "There are wonderful things coming. Coming very soon in your life. Big changes."

Emma's brow furrowed. She turned toward Daniel, puzzled by Amira's cryptic words, but found him watching the two women with a surprised smile.

A shadow fell across the low table, and Emma looked up to see Mohammed, the desert expedition guide. His dark blue djellaba swept the floor as he settled onto a pouf beside her and Daniel.

"Everything is ready," Mohammed said to Daniel in careful English. His weathered face creased into a smile.

Emma's fork paused halfway to her mouth. "Ready?" She looked from Mohammed to Daniel. "What does he mean?"

Daniel's eyes sparkled and he shot a quick glance to Amira. "Remember how I've been disappearing these past couple days?"

Emma set down her fork. "Did you think I could forget that you were off investigating without me?"

Daniel shook his head. "Not investigating. I was planning something special." He reached for her hand. "Mohammed has helped me arrange a trip for us into the Sahara. We leave tomorrow morning."

"The desert?" Emma nearly spilled her water glass. "Really?"

"Camels, Bedouin tents, the whole experience," Daniel squeezed her fingers.

"Oh, how marvelous!" Edith clapped her hands together. "Just like my expedition! Though do watch out for scorpions in your shoes. Nasty creatures."

The evening call to prayer drifted through the open windows, the muezzin's melodic voice echoing across the rooftops of the medina.

Mohammed said something in Arabic and Khadija hurried over to translate.

"You'll see the sunset over the dunes," Khadija said. "Very beautiful. Like fire in the sky."

Emma turned to Daniel. "So this is what you've been working on? Not avoiding me during the investigation?"

"You were handling that brilliantly on your own." Daniel grinned. "I just wanted to surprise you."

"Next time, just tell me you're planning something nice." Emma bumped his shoulder with hers. "So I don't worry you're shutting me out again."

"Deal." Daniel kissed her temple.

"The stars," Fatima said softly from across the table. "You won't believe how many stars you can see out there."

"And the silence," Brian added. "It's like nothing else on earth."

Mina appeared with fresh mint tea, and Mustafa poured it from high above the glasses in the traditional style. Fragrant steam swirled in the lantern light.

"When do we leave?" Emma asked, accepting a glass of the sweet tea.

"Dawn," Mohammed replied. "The desert waits for no one."

"You must tell us all about it when you return," Edith insisted as she held up the key she had finally located in the pocket of her flowered dress. "Every detail!"

Epilogue

The Land Rover bumped across the rocky desert terrain as dawn painted the sky in shades of rose and gold. Emma braced herself against the door, watching the landscape change from city to scrubland to endless waves of sand.

"Look!" She pointed to a cluster of camels in the distance, their shapes dark against the brightening horizon.

Daniel shifted closer. "Those are ours."

The vehicle pulled up beside a group of men in blue robes who stood with the camels. Mohammed jumped out and greeted them in rapid Arabic.

Emma eyed the towering animals. "They're bigger than I expected."

"Here." One of the men gestured for Emma to put her foot in his linked hands. She gripped the wooden saddle and let him boost her up. The camel lurched to its feet, rear legs first, pitching her forward.

"Oh!" She clutched the pommel. "This is... different!"

Daniel chuckled as he mounted his own camel with an equal lack of grace. He nearly toppled off as the camel stood. "You okay over there?"

"Ask me again in an hour."

They set off across the dunes in a line, their camels' feet silent in the sand. The morning air held a surprising chill, and Emma pulled her light jacket closer. As the sun climbed higher, the desert transformed into a sea of gold.

"It's like being on another planet," she called to Daniel.

He nodded, adjusting his sunglasses. "Makes Whispering Pines seem very far away."

They stopped for lunch in the shade of an acacia tree. Mohammed and his team spread carpets on the sand and unpacked containers of olives, fresh bread, and dried fruit.

"The bread is still warm." Emma broke off a piece. "How do they do that?"

"Ancient desert magic," Daniel winked.

"Or maybe solar heat on the camel bags." Emma winked back.

By late afternoon, they reached the camp. Striped Bedouin tents stood in a half circle, their sides lifted to catch any breeze. Inside, Emma found thick rugs layered on the sand and cushions and poufs piled against low divans.

"This isn't exactly roughing it," she said, running her hand over an embroidered pillow.

"Glamping, Moroccan style."

As the sun began to set, their guides lit brass lanterns that cast dancing shadows on the tent walls. The aroma of spices drifted from the cooking fire where a tagine bubbled.

212

"Smell that?" Emma closed her eyes. "Saffron and… something caramely."

They gathered around low tables set with steaming plates of couscous studded with vegetables and tender lamb. Emma pulled a piece of sh'bakia from a platter.

"I know how to make these now," she whispered to Daniel with a grin. "In case you wondered."

"Planning to add Moroccan pastries to the bakery menu?"

"Maybe. Though I'm not sure Whispering Pines is ready for orange honey-soaked sesame cookies."

One of the guides brought out an oud, its pear-shaped body gleaming in the firelight. As he began to play, the desert night filled with haunting melodies and Emma remembered Karim on their first night in Marrakesh. Stars appeared one by one until the sky blazed with light.

"I've never seen so many stars," Emma breathed.

Daniel wrapped an arm around her shoulders. "Worth the camel ride?"

"Worth every sore muscle." She leaned against him. "Though my leg muscles might say something different tomorrow."

The music continued as mint tea was poured from silver pots held high above tiny glasses, the liquid falling in a thin stream that created a crown of foam.

Hours later, a gentle touch on her shoulder pulled Emma from sleep. Daniel's silhouette blocked the lantern light filtering through the tent walls.

"Come with me." His voice was soft. "There's something you need to see."

Emma shook her sandals to check for scorpions, then slipped her feet into them and followed him out of the tent. The desert air held a pre-dawn chill that made her shiver. Daniel took her hand and led her up the nearest dune.

"Watch your step." He steadied her as loose sand shifted beneath her feet.

At the crest, Emma caught her breath. The sky stretched endless above them, a tapestry of stars so bright and numerous they seemed to crowd each other out, close enough to touch.

"Oh my gosh," she breathed. "It's like diamond dust scattered across the universe." She turned in a slow circle, taking in the full sweep of the horizon.

"Beautiful, isn't it?" Daniel's voice had an odd catch to it. "But not as beautiful as you."

Emma turned back to find him down on one knee in the sand, holding up a small box. The stars seemed to spin around her as she realized what was happening.

"Oh!" Her hand flew to her mouth.

"Remember when you spotted me at the gem shop?" Daniel's blue eyes caught the starlight. "I was looking at rings. I wanted to find something perfect, because you're perfect for me."

He opened the box to reveal a delicate ring that sparkled even in the darkness.

"Emma Harper, will you marry me?"

She dropped to her knees in front of him and threw her arms around his neck. "There's no one I'd rather solve murders with, bake sweets for, and be married to, than you."

"Is that a yes?" His arms tightened around her.

"Yes! A thousand times yes!"

He slipped the ring onto her finger just as the first rays of dawn spilled over the dunes.

When he kissed her, Emma felt her heart soar.

Visit Penelope Online
to read all her book directly from the author,
get free books, and more!

www.PenelopeLoveletter.com

lots of love,

Penelope

Made in the USA
Columbia, SC
18 January 2025

52103180R00136